NEITHER

Rakhshanda Jalil (b. 1963) has translated a collection of Premchand's short stories entitled *The Temple and the Mosque* (HarperCollins, 1992); edited an anthology of Urdu short stories, called *Urdu Stories* (Srishti, 2002); *Lies: Half Told* (Srishti, 2002), translated a collection of satirical writings in Hindi by Asghar Wajahat; *Black Borders*, 32 satirical cameos by Saadat Hasan Manto (Rupa & Co., 2003); *Through the Closed Doorway*, nazms by Urdu poet Shahryar (Rupa & Co., 2004); *Circle and Other Stories* by Intizar Hussain (Rupa & Co., 2004) and *A Winter's Tale & Other Stories,* a collection of Premchand's short stories for children (Puffin, 2007). Her translations have appeared in *The India International Centre Quarterly, The Little Magazine, The Week, The Annual of Urdu Studies* and *Indian Literature* among others. She has recently co-authored *Partners in Freedom: Jamia Millia Islamia* (Niyogi, 2006) and written *Invisible City*, a collection of essays on the little-known monuments of Delhi (Niyogi, forthcoming).

Rakhshanda Jalil has taught English at the universities of Delhi and Aligarh. Presently, she works as Media and Cultural Coordinator at Jamia Millia Islamia.

NEITHER NIGHT NOR DAY

Thirteen Stories by Women from Pakistan

Edited by
Rakhshanda Jalil

HarperCollins *Publishers* India

a joint venture with

New Delhi

First published in India in 2007 by
HarperCollins *Publishers* India
a joint venture with
The India Today Group

Anthology Copyright © HarperCollins *Publishers* India 2007
Introduction Copyright © Rakhshanda Jalil

ISBN 13-978-81-7223-691-5

HarperCollins *Publishers*
1A Hamilton House, Connaught Place, New Delhi 110001, India
77-85 Fulham Palace Road, London W6 8JB, United Kingdom
Hazelton Lanes, 55 Avenue Road, Suite 2900, Toronto, Ontario M5R 3L2
and 1995 Markham Road, Scarborough, Ontario M1B 5M8, Canada
25 Ryde Road, Pymble, Sydney, NSW 2073, Australia
31 View Road, Glenfield, Auckland 10, New Zealand
10 East 53rd Street, New York NY 10022, USA

Typeset in 13/15 AmericanGaramond
Mindways Design

Printed and bound at
Thomson Press (India) Ltd.

For my mother, Mehjabeen Jalil

Contents

Introduction

The exchange of literatures between India and Pakistan has traditionally adopted a circuitous route. Usually through the West, it takes place with one eye firmly on the gallery of western critics and the other on the pantheon of literary agents. Sadly, it is governed more by current literary fads than any real interest in seeing literature as a mirror of society. In the early eighties, when Salman Rushdie opened the doors to a new world of magic realism, causing a near-deluge of fantastical writing, he spawned a generation of wannabes. Then came a near obsessive-compulsive soul-searching on the Partition and the writings of Saadat Hasan Manto, Ashfaq Ahmad, Intizar Hussain suddenly found avid readers and ready publishers. In Urdu, the interest has almost entirely been in poetry, and that too the ghazal. Collections by Faiz Ahmad Faiz, Habib Jalib, Ahmad Faraz have been pirated and sold not just in Urdu but also in Devnagari in equally large numbers.

In the case of women's writing, this exchange has been marked more by stereotyping than a genuine curiosity about each other's lives. These few and far-between exchanges – again through the West, again largely through the English language – dwell on a sense of 'otherness', choosing to highlight the exotic rather than the ordinary, giving preference to voices of dissent and discontent rather than those that speak of the small joys and sorrows. In Pakistan, women who write in English are often charged with writing for a small incestuous group that is far removed from the 'real' Pakistan. Disparaged as elitist and accused of suffering from a colonial hangover and a West-fixation, Pakistani women writers have, therefore, traditionally found themselves doubly marginalized. Save for a lone Bapsi Sidhwa and in later years Kamila Shamsie and Sara Suleri who have found ready publishers and eager audiences abroad before becoming 'known' in their own country, not much is known or read of contemporary women writers from Pakistan. The precious little that is available – as stray articles through the internet or in anthologies – is usually overtly 'feminist' and concerned exclusively with issues of gender, space and identity.

The discerning reader – be it in India, Pakistan or in the West – wants to read writings from Pakistan that are contemporary, diverse and reflective of Pakistani society, its aspirations and dynamics. While it isn't possible for most of us in India to access these literatures in their Urdu and Punjabi versions let alone Sindhi, Baluchi, Pashto originals, and English perforce becomes the link language, one does seek voices that mirror regional variations – both in terms of style and content. And so, when we talk of literature from Pakistan, it is important to remember that, like India, Pakistan is not a homogenous monolithic bloc – linguistically or culturally – and its literatures reflect this pluralism.

While any selection of writing is, by its very nature, a subjective exercise, my criteria have been somewhat pedestrian. In setting out to compile this selection of short stories, I must confess I chose Ordinariness as my anthem, for I believe that by celebrating ordinariness we celebrate life as it is lived by scores of real people. Indeed, there is much to be said for the Commonplace for it is often a reliable barometer of a society and its people.

My concern in this book, therefore, has been to present as complete a picture of the everydayness of life as it is lived and experienced by Pakistani women. The majority of writers chosen here actually live in Pakistan; others who live or work abroad have maintained close links with their country. The criteria for selection rests not so much on name or fame or technical virtuosity in the craft of the short story but on telling as many stories as possible in as many styles and voices as possible. And so there is Nayyara Rahman speaking with a heart-felt earnestness of a young single mother's search for a job in 'The Job Application'. Sabyn Javeri-Jillani writes with candour of being suspended between cultures, between spaces, and the fear of slipping through the cracks that differentiate the eastern and western way of life lends a poignant urgency to her writing. It is only by writing, by putting her feelings in black and white that a young writer taking her first uncertain steps in two worlds — that of writing and of settling down to a new life in the West — can give any coherence to her jumbled feelings.

Many of the stories included here are by young and relatively less known writers. A couple of them are the sort you are likely to come across in popular digests but the freshness of their approach and the note of authenticity that rings out loud and clear makes them eminently suitable for selection. Hopefully, readers will find it refreshing not to come across the usual names that are most anthologized and therefore, erroneously, taken as being representative. The writers in this collection mirror, each in her own unique way, events that are known and familiar to them. That the events may sometimes be perfectly ordinary in no way detracts from their readability.

Stories appear in the alphabetical order of the author's last name. There is no grand design in the sequence; given the entirely personal and completely subjective selection, it seemed simpler to free the reader from the snare of attempting to follow some sort of narrative. Let me confess there is none. Of the thirteen stories, nine are based in cities or deal with an urban setting, the rest have a rural milieu. Fantasies, memoirs, near-autobiographical accounts, even a good old-fashioned put-your-hair-on-end ghost story as well as 'realist' story-telling — this is a mixed bag, one that will hopefully yield something of interest to readers regardless of gender. I never cease to marvel why anthologies by women writers put together by women editors assume that the subject matter of their selection must be of over-powering interest to women alone. I must confess that I find such assumptions as bizarre as assuming that dalit writing is only for dalit readers, or black writing exclusively for a black audience.

And so you will find within these pages Sehba Sarwar using the conventions of a simplistic ghost story, with all its accompanying paraphernalia such as a rattling-creaking-groaning elevator and a wild-eyed spectre in a red gharara, as props to locate her story and talk of a Karachi where both Hindus and Muslims lived together. Narrated by a precocious teenager, the story becomes first a discovery and then a lament for a shared past. The shared fabric of Pakistani society about to be torn apart by communal hatred is revealed also in Sorayya Khan's 'Five Queen's Street'. The only extract in this anthology, it too has a young female protagonist who witnesses the abduction of her Hindu neighbour and expresses outrage as only the young can. Zahida Hina writes about a mother on death row walking the last few steps towards her execution while her little boy clings to her in sleep. Why is she being executed? What is her sin? And who is she, for that matter? Nothing is told, for nothing matters in the last few moments before death. Qaisra Shahraz spins a powerful tale of a son first shunning, then reclaiming his deaf-mute father who has been cast in the role of the village idiot all his life. Nikhat Hasan writes about a land of dumb people whose citizens are not born dumb but whose tongues are severed at birth in a barbaric rite aimed at increasing productivity and industriousness. But, as the country's ruler – the only person in the kingdom who has a tongue and that too nine yards long – discovers, one can silence tongues but not the will of people. Are these stories of interest only to women simply because they are written by women? I think not.

While some of these stories have been translated into English, others have been written originally in English, demonstrating how English has been naturalized and adapted to serve indigenous needs and in the process created a literature that is modern and relevant. Interestingly enough, these writers use English with effortless ease to talk of issues that are, in a sense, completely non-English, or at the very least not-quite-Western. Bina Shah describes a frontier wedding that begins like any wedding in any rural outpost anywhere in the world but ends with the brutal honour killing of the bride. Soniah Kamal too uses language as a tool to tell a macabre tale of female foeticide and the terrible price that women who defy patriarchal norms in a closed society must pay. She uses the very English style of understatement to devastating effect, creating a crisp, crackling little tale that relies on brevity to carry its sting and make its final denouement against a system that demands a woman's breast as price for feeding a new-born baby girl in defiance of a tribunal's orders that baby girls must necessarily be buried unless and until there is a male baby of the same age group who can one day marry her. Soniah Kamal's terse storytelling carries a chilling comment on a society that views women merely as receptacles to beget male heirs.

A book such as this will, hopefully, meet the needs and interests of a wide variety of readers: of those engaged in women's studies in South Asia, particularly Pakistan, students of South Asian literature, as well as people from the South Asian diaspora who look upon the literature from this part of the world as a part of their cultural heritage but use English as their effective first language. It would, of course, be a bonus if those who know little or nothing of the literature from Pakistan can find in this book a starting point, something that engages their interest and drives them to read more. It will also, one hopes, dispel the entirely erroneous notion that nothing of any particular merit is being written by contemporary writers on both sides of the border.

Rakhshanda Jalil
June 2007
New Delhi

Plans in Pink

Kiran Bashir Ahmad

Heaven Apartments were painted pink. Perhaps the builder had the pale tints of sunrise in mind when he built them. But no matter what rationale one chose to give, the fact remained that there they stood – tall, stark and solid – through three years of glaring sun, lashing rain, vehicles spewing smoke on one of Karachi's major arteries, and the seepage from numerous leaking bathrooms creating its own design. They were now a bright gaudy pink, resembling the colour of a tomboyish girl's kameez that had been unwashed for over a week. The girl – she had a definite role or rather, would have a definite role...but for now – the colour...

On a more positive note, the colour did distinguish the long line of apartments from the other grey, brown or white structures in the vicinity, which was exactly what Samina had in mind while explaining the address somewhat hurriedly to her daughter's tutor. What could a working woman do when literally everything had to be done on a Sunday – cooking for the week, doing the previous week's laundry and so on.

'It is pink!' she had been forced to scream into the receiver through the increasing noise of the static.

'What – stink?' asked Valerie in a rather confused voice.

The message had finally got through after a moment of sheepish embarrassment on either end of the line, and now Valerie was putting down the receiver, chewing on her stub of pencil like a meditative calf, as her eyes took in the chaos of the once neat and tidy room where numerous students had diligently learnt their 'oh-so-difficult English lessons'. She could almost picture Ali and Mishal, or Al and Mish as her mother had liked to call the twins, sitting together on the cushy sofa below the window and reciting Wordsworth's 'Daffodils'. It was a poem usually reserved for the tenth graders at which level it was taught in their school, but Valerie chose to make an exception in this case, as the twins proved to be an exceptionally bright pair. At twelve years, they understood the various nuances of rhyme as well as, if not better than, the dull ninth and tenth graders she usually tutored.

It was their mother, Mrs Samina Tariq, she had been talking to. A good natured, helpful and inordinately stupid woman was Valerie's first impression of her. And now, as she surveyed her flight schedule yet again, she smiled and hummed to herself, happy that her guess had been correct. Though how on earth her mother would manage to stay on in Samina's house for a whole year was a mystery Valerie chose not to dwell on. It was causing her a headache, plus the thought – the very thought of finally being independent – was overwhelming. 'Yes, better not think about it.' She chose instead to think of Sam…Sam – Samina, back to Samina. Valerie could remember the look on Samina's face when her mother had tried to call Samina 'Sam'. She laughed to herself. Apart from that first blunder, things had gone smoothly.

Samina had been a gem. 'Of course!' she had gushed. 'I can understand how difficult it is for you now that you are going to Australia. Don't you worry. She can stay with me till she puts things in order here and joins you.'

'It'll only take around two or three weeks, I'm sure.' Valerie had beamed at her.

'Oh, she's more than welcome! I will look after your mother like my own. The children can sleep with me...so much the better since Tariq isn't here...' But that was all that Valerie had heard or had needed to hear, she was already far away, blissful in her thoughts of Australia where somewhere Sunnysam, as his nickname on the net proclaimed, was waiting for her as he himself put it, 'breathlessly, as if on the edge of a diving board.' Valerie could almost picture his muscular and fully toned body in the pair of swimming trunks she had sent him along with a few other toiletries a month after their online relationship had commenced, thanks to one of the more popular Christian dating websites, and a week after, he had told her that he was serious in his intentions and wanted to marry her. She had sent him the trunks and had in return received a box of twelve long-stemmed roses: white with a blush of crimson at the edges.

Mrs D' Souza had been unexpectedly encouraging. Valerie looked at the ticket again – Valerie D' Souza was printed neatly on top – a one-way ticket to the land Down Under. With luck, she would never have to bear with her mother's foibles again, not for a year at least, when she would have to arrange for her to come to

Australia. That was her mother's plan, but in the meantime, Valerie hoped that she would be able to locate a comfortable old people's home.

I was looking into the mirror on my cupboard, and all I could see of Valerie was her shiny black hair, and yet I knew that she was thinking about the future. Future: the word came fully loaded – expectations, responsibilities and desires, but above all, uncertainty. I wondered whether I had done the right thing in allowing her to dream, then shrugged the troubling thought out of my mind. Had I ever been wrong? And Valerie, after all, was my daughter. She could take care of herself. I was sure of that. Hadn't she twisted Samina round her little finger? Granted, I had guided her, but she had managed the last part quite well. I was sure that she would be able to do the same with Sam. Once she had the nationality, there would be no need of him. There was one problem though. She said she loved him. Love over what? A computer? I was sure, as I pinned up my grey hair in the pink butterfly clip, that all that love would go right out of the swimming pool once Valerie had a chance to compare a Pakistani-Australian banker's lifestyle with that of her beloved swimmer. That the said banker, James, was also from our community made the package more attractive.

One part of my plan was complete. The house was sold, I had a place to stay, and Valerie had her ticket. Now I only had to see her off and then land up two weeks later in Australia myself, unknown to anyone but James, and of course Samina. Come to think of it, the only one who did not know that my so-called lie to Samina was actually the truth, was Valerie! She would thank me later. Plus, I could always say that I meant it to be a surprise. Did she think I was actually going to stay on here like the rest of them – the greying old wives of greying old remnants of the sixties? An unsightly lot I found them, ambling forward wearily like turtles, poking their sticks here and there nervously like mice scuttling the ground as they walked up the drive of the Grand Club periodically, to play the same old Mah-jong or chess or bridge – oh, they were all so alike! Dull people with dull lives. The Lord alone knew how long I would live and as long as I did, I wanted to see the world and secure my youngest daughter a good future as I had done with Melanie. Wasn't Melanie now living securely in Canada where her husband – also one of my discoveries in the community – worked in the oil fields? The thought was intensely comforting, like a woolly blanket on this cold December night. She had also considered herself to be smitten by that fellow…what-was-his-name-now…It would be history repeating itself, nothing more.

The scrawny ginger and black speckled cat arched its back and tried to dive deeper into the rotting pile of rubbish beside a wall from which the pink paint was slowly peeling off. Its tail lashed out against the brutality of this cold December day. That its nameless and homeless existence would soon be changed by the arrival of a burly middle-aged woman dressed in pink much like the walls of the apartment was a matter far beyond its comprehension – for the moment at least.

Peering out of the window of her third-floor apartment in anticipation of her guest, Samina had a much better idea, that's what she thought in any case, of the road along which things were to proceed. She had met Valerie's mother, Mrs D' Souza…come to think of it, she did not even know her first name…on two occasions only, and had summed her up as a sweet old thing. A bit batty surely, but no harm in her. Her arrival would create quite a stir in the neighbourhood, but for her purposes, Mrs D' Souza was the ideal person. After all, where else could she find someone who could manage her children in these winter vacations while she went out to work? She was sure that Valerie's mother would prove to be an excellent housekeeper as well. Her first aim surely was to make her postpone her flight and if that failed, then a delay could always be manufactured.

The group of rag pickers stood staring at the gate, looks of mingled shock and awe writ large on their grimy faces. They stood staring for a minute, and then as if on cue, started sniggering at the sight of an old woman wearing… Could it be? A dress! They moved over gingerly to the boundary wall of the rubbish dump outlining the apartment blocks for a closer look.

'She's a memsahib!' said one, awestruck, slipping over the stinking mound barefoot in his hurry to get a glimpse of her legs.

'You're an idiot!' said one of the older boys, cuffing him on the head with the younger one's rubber slipper, which had fallen at his feet. He pulled him up. 'Look at her face!' he said knowingly. 'She can't be one. Get back to work now.' The younger one was silenced and an assortment of cuffs and blows was enough to persuade the rest to resume their work. It would be much later in the evening when they sat on their haunches in front of Qalandar's restaurant waiting for someone to donate food, that he would find out from the cart pushers of the area that she indeed was a foreigner by heritage and a non-Muslim too.

For now, he stole fervent sidelong glances at this new find as the group rummaged in the dump for paper, broken shards of glass and even edible titbits for a change of taste.

'Meow!' The speckled cat was sniffing expectantly at his gunny bag.

He threw a stone at it, which caught it on the leg. It meowed loudly and piteously.

It was this movement and then the meow that followed, which drew my attention to the park beside the gate. Before this, I had been surveying the line of apartments in front of me while the taxi driver removed my luggage.

'Yes, they are pink,' I was thinking, 'and yes, there is a stink too!' The pink heaven stood tall before me, made more colourful by the washing that billowed gently from almost all the balconies.

Heaven Apartments indeed! The rotting rubbish in front, the ragged little boys playing cricket on the mangy patch of land, the rag pickers sifting through the dump, and the peeling paint outlined by yellowing pipes, made it look more like something out of a 'Reality Bites' TV show! I nostalgically thought of my own comfortable flat which had been sold off by now, and of Valerie's tears when I had stopped her from taking the lift up to see it one more time. That girl did have a tendency to get emotional. Just like her father, God bless him.

'Let bygones be bygones,' I had told her as I held her back. 'Look towards the future!'

I had led her to the radio cab and we said our goodbyes at the airport – Valerie's teary and mine, calm. Couldn't really blame her for that, of course. She had no idea that she would be seeing me sooner than she expected.

I had spent the last few days packing my stuff, and this morning, had handed over the keys of the apartment to the new owners. Now, I smiled at my own joke as I stood outside my temporary 'heaven-cum-haven'. This would be the final goodbye to my numbered days in Karachi.

All this and more was in my mind as I walked across the ground, past the little urchins staring at me quite openly, to where the rag pickers stood with their sacks over their shoulders, also staring unabashedly. Nothing new for me; I knew they had few chances of seeing a woman's legs and here I was, providing them with every opportunity to do so. The uncouth little brats! I admonished the one before me for hitting the cat and picked up the limping creature using the handkerchief which till then I had been holding to my nose. I have always loved animals. At one time, I had eight cats and two children, all in one flat. To see one in pain and move on would have been unthinkable. I carried it with me, still feeling their eyes on my back.

'No use,' I told myself, 'some people never learn.'

Samina had been watching the entire scene from above. She looked alarmed. She hadn't bargained on a cat entering the fray! This would have to be dealt with, was her foremost thought as she left the window and headed for the door.

Flat number 20-C was the second apartment. I gave the rest a cursory look and signalled the driver to bring my luggage. Samina met me at the foot of the stairs. I had been framing the right words for a greeting when her shriek startled me. Her eyes were resting on the cat cradled in my arms. I held out my hand in greeting and she started to sneeze, gesturing at the cat, which now seemed poised to jump out and run away. I started to explain but there was a clatter above us, and Mish's braided hair bobbed into view. A moment later she had hugged me, kissed me and taken the cat from me with many ohs and ahs of concern. I smiled at her and felt the tension disappear from the corners of my lips.

'See, you and me…same, same Pinky auntie!' she said, tugging at her kameez and then my dress and indicating the colour.

Samina had stopped sneezing. I don't know how else to describe it but when I looked into her eyes, which held a relenting look now, I had the uncanny feeling that I was being judged.

It was on the third day of my stay with the family that Samina asked me how long I planned to stay with them. I was surprised at the question but didn't show it.

'I told you my ticket is booked for the twenty-first of December. I want to be with Valerie on Christmas,' I said.

She looked disappointed. 'I'm quite delighted to have you here, you know, and so are the children, and you did say that Valerie is going to meet her fiancé. Don't you think she could do with a little more time on her own?'

'Good Lord!' I thought to myself, 'Does she really mean to saddle me with her children and the house while she goes out to work? How preposterous!' My definite refusal was taken quite calmly. A bit too calmly, I felt. Samina nodded, pressed my hand gently and expressed her regret.

A day before I was to leave, I had my luggage ready. It was dark when I decided to check the exact time of departure of my flight so that I could call for a radio cab for the airport. That's when I found that the ticket had simply disappeared. Twenty-first of December – the day I was supposed to leave in a radio cab – I left in an ambulance. I had had a heart attack.

Gloria Park. The plaque still adorns the gate of a certain pink boundary wall. If you bother to ask the children playing inside about the unusual foreign name in an obviously conservative Muslim mohalla, they will tell you quite boastfully that it was one of their Pinky auntie's influential friends who got the rubbish dump converted into a park for the sole purpose of allowing her young and inexperienced teenage attendant to guide her wheelchair in the open for much needed fresh air in the evenings. And that Gloria was Pinky auntie's first name which she put on the plaque as a tribute to her love for gardening. If you ask where you can meet her, they will point upwards and say, in heaven.

Pinky auntie must have been quite a favourite, you will observe, for the children look both eager and bashful when questioned about her. Further questioning will reveal that she used to sit with them at night and tell them stories of princes and princesses and far-away lands. The flat she lived in was filled with uncles and aunties all the time, and they would have taken her away if Mish baji, as the children call her in respect, had not become so upset at the thought of losing her friend. You will learn that she did lose her ultimately, as Pinky auntie passed away a month after her heart attack.

There is a ginger and black speckled cat watching you as you listen to all this. At night, when the children have ceased playing, it goes and looks for scraps under the benches lining the boundary wall. Sometimes it finds something and sometimes it doesn't, but either way it simply curls up near the place where the rubbish dump used to be, and waits for pink lines to outline the edge of the night. Around this time, a girl with long plaits swinging behind her comes running to the edge of the park with leftovers and runs away hurriedly after giving it a swift pat on the head.

Far away in another land across the oceans, another similarly speckled but well fed cat sleeps peacefully on a rug as Valerie strokes it gently and thinks of her mother who loved cats so much.

The Tongue

Nikhat Hasan

It was a land of dumb people. Its citizens weren't born dumb, though. Going by the edict of its ruler, the tongue of every newborn baby was severed at the root. In the middle of the city, there was a little mound of severed tongues. This mound was guarded by an old bearded man who wore a garland of severed tongues; his eyes were small and round, and his nose quite flat. One could see all his teeth through his gaping mouth from far away. All day, he sat quietly on a stool while people dumped severed tongues on the mound from large baskets. For a little while, the small red tongues squirmed on the mound, and then turned into lifeless lumps of flesh. No one knew if the guard had a tongue in his mouth since no one had ever heard him talk.

The citizens were doing well. They didn't have that look of despair that mutes generally have. All day long, they worked without speaking, and they worked four times as fast as ordinary people. Their ruler was a young boy. Every morning, he went out to inspect his people as they worked like machines or cattle, and nodded his head in silent approval. On his shoulder, folded into loops, hung his own tongue, nine yards long. This was a family trait. His father had a long tongue and, they said, so had his father's father. The family of long-tongued people had been ruling the country for centuries. Safian, the young ruler, was still a bachelor and had no intention of getting married in the near future. He wanted to introduce a few important changes in his kingdom. His vision was to revise the outdated administrative structure of the government. The notion of making these changes occurred to him one day when he saw the guard's daughter. This girl, fourteen or fifteen years old, was talking non-stop despite not having a tongue. She came to the mound carrying lunch for her father, and after dumping the box on the ground, started babbling. She was opposed to the established ways of the country and wanted to warn the ruler of the dire consequences of the barbaric rite. It was then that Safian realized that she could not be silenced even though her tongue had been cut off at its root. This girl was speaking even without her tongue, and the sounds she emitted were more dreadful than ordinary sounds. Safian asked the guard about the most recently severed tongues, and in response to the old man's gestures went behind the mound. He found several large baskets filled with severed tongues. Blood was leaching from the baskets and clotting on the ground. For some time, Safian stood quiet, looking at the tongues. Far off in the fields, dumb people were busy at their work. The farmers had broad chests, and their strong muscles rippled under the strain.

Safian wandered for hours in the densely populated areas of his country. He took his tongue from his shoulder and draped it over his arm. Then he coiled it around his neck. He was sick to death of his tongue. Many times he had made up his mind to have it cut, but it was his heritage. Besides, a ruler had to have a long tongue. Safian often advised his subjects about the evils of the tongue. There was a time when everyone had a foot-long tongue which wagged all the time. The endless wagging of these tongues had brought the country bad luck. Crops began to rot before they could be harvested. Sometimes there were famines, sometimes plagues, sometimes the horrors of war. At other times, murders and gushing rivers of blood. In those times, the citizens used nothing but their tongues. They hurled verbal abuses at one another and constantly quarrelled among themselves. Minor differences grew into civil wars. The country was ruled by Safian's ancestor, the long-tongued Khaldoom. He was an experienced ruler with great foresight. He could not bear to see the plight of his country. Whenever he saw human beings fighting like quarrelsome cocks, he brooded. From the fields, he returned even sadder. Frost-bitten crops and dusty fields seemed to be crying out at the ineptitude of man.

'Why don't my citizens work?' he asked himself.

'They are afflicted with the deadly disease of talking. This disease has grown into an epidemic. They will not mend their ways until …' Khaldoom suddenly leapt at the solution. He called his special attendant, who was throwing stones at passers-by. The attendant came in and started to speak incessantly.

'Quiet, quiet!' screamed Khaldoom and in his anger, pulled the attendant's tongue out by the root. A fountain of blood gushed forth from his mouth. Khaldoom was gripped by madness. Completely out of his senses, he ordered that the tongues of all citizens be severed at the root. Hearing this order, all the citizens fled the country, except for a few women. In time, these women gave birth to three children, who were presented to Khaldoom. Seeing the children cry and scream, Khaldoom was gripped by the same madness once again. 'Damn, evil, evil, damn,' he cried and ordered the tongues of the children to be cut off. Soon, the rite became the law in the country. After ridding themselves of the evil of the tongue, the citizens prospered beyond belief. By the time Khaldoom died, the country's population had tripled, and all the people were dumb, completely free from the evils of the tongue. They did not know how to speak. All day long, they worked like machines or cattle.

These days, however, the country was rife with whispering campaigns. Out on his inspections, Safian heard a murmur like the buzzing of flies. Work had slowed down. The old curse was slowly descending again, seeping in little by little. Safian was puzzled. The region still had the same age-old laws. He had considered changes in the old administrative system, but had not yet started implementing them. Then he saw Sarah, the daughter of the guard. Even without a tongue, she was chattering non-stop. Her eyes, nose and ears were expressive beyond belief. Safian was both angry and surprised. He walked behind the mound, where large baskets lay full of freshly severed tongues. Sarah was laughing uncontrollably. Seeing Safian coming towards her, she opened her deep-well mouth and laughed like a mad woman. Safian saw something peeping out of the back of her mouth. When he went closer to see what it was, she scrambled up the mound. Something was still fluttering inside her mouth. Safian walked towards the front of the mound, where the guard sat on a stool, his head bowed. He shouted at the guard in a voice like thunder. The guard trembled with fear but when he opened his mouth to say something, out fell his tongue, which had been stuck to the roof of his mouth. Then, in a quavering voice, the guard begged Safian to order all the citizens to open their mouths.

By evening, as darkness fell over the land, every single citizen in the country stood before Safian to show his gaping mouth. Safian was dumbfounded to discover that in every mouth, the root of the severed tongue was slowly growing back into the shape of a tongue.

Translated from the Urdu by BAIDAR BAKHT *and*
KATHLEEN GRANT JAEGER

She Who Went Looking for Butterflies

Zahida Hina

Narjis saw white-haired Amma sitting outside the prison door. Tears were flowing from her eyes. Bhaiyya's head was bent. She could not see his face from this distance. Mehdi clapped his hands and laughed aloud. Then he stuck his hands out of the prison bars. 'Mama, my toffees,' he chattered.

Her brother raised his head and took Mehdi's hands in his. His tears tried vainly to wash Mehdi's soiled hands. Like other good and bad scenes, Narjis stored this one too in her memory. She felt somewhat comforted; when Amma was no more, at least there would be someone to take care of Mehdi. Bhaiyya loved Mehdi dearly and would certainly take care of him.

Bhaiyya had begged her time and again to sign the papers for an appeal for mercy, but failed to make her yield. The deadline for the appeal had passed and now she stood face to face with death. Amma clung to her hand like a swimmer grasps the hand of a drowning person. Her touch spoke of helplessness, separation and immeasurable grief. This would be Narjis's last touch from the outside world – a world that was filled with beauty and ugliness, goodness and evil, love and hatred.

Mehdi kept chuckling merrily. He was chattering with Bhaiyya. Sometimes he would wriggle his little face out of the bars and kiss Mama's face, sometimes he would play with his grandmother's hair.

Amma was happy that Mehdi would be free from prison. What had he seen beyond prison bars, handcuffs, chains and bayonets! He was born here and these barracks had been his entire world so far. Now, he would be able to go to school, to the bazaar, and play in the garden.

'Bhaiyya, you must put him on a swing.'

'Aapa, in the name of God and the Prophet, be quiet.' Bhaiyya began to sob and she became quiet.

She could understand Amma's and Bhaiyya's agony, but she was unable to make them understand that sometimes one chooses death for oneself so that others may live. She and Haseen had been taken into police custody together. Then came the news that Haseen had committed suicide during interrogation. She knew that when prisoners taken by the army could not stand the torture and died, their bodies were not given to their kin. They would lie in unmarked graves and the death of such victims was labelled as suicide by their murderers. He too was a prisoner of conscience like her, and prisoners of conscience do not commit suicide, nor do they beg for mercy.

When the time for this last meeting was over, Amma fainted. Bhaiyya clung to the prison bars. He was kissing her hands and touching her hair. Then they left. No, they did not leave; they were forced to leave. Narjis longed to embrace Bhaiyya for the last time, but it was not possible. The rules of the jail had been made by human beings, but human relations and human sentiments had no place in the rulebook. When Mama left, Mehdi began to howl. He wanted to go to the place that Ammi talked about in her stories. But Ammi never allowed him to go anywhere.

'You will be allowed to go tomorrow. Mama will take you with him.'

Narjis began kissing Mehdi's cheeks. Warden Maryam glanced at the mother and son and lowered her head.

What kind of a woman was this, who had not challenged the death sentence by appealing for mercy, who had not shed a tear on entering the death cell, neither screamed nor cursed God or the jailor or anyone? When the Quran was given to her, she lifted it to her eyes for a brief moment and put it aside, and then continued to kiss her son. When maulvi sahib asked her to beg forgiveness from God, she kept smiling. When he left, she put away the prayer mat under her pillow, lay down and began to tell stories to her son.

The female ward was filled with all sorts of women, convicted or accused. Not one among them felt that Narjis was like them. These 'bad' women had treated her very well in the past four years, though she was beyond their understanding. Perhaps that was why they loved, respected and, at the same time, feared her. They could not understand why she was being given such a severe punishment if she had not slandered anyone, nor stolen anyone's cattle, nor dealt in country liquor or drugs, nor murdered anyone.

'Bibi, are you not afraid?' Maryam had asked her a few days after she was transferred to the death cell.

'Afraid of what?' Narjis's voice was devoid of any anxiety.

'Of death?'

'No, when one is in control of death, it holds no fear. And Mehdi is there too. He will survive me and I will survive in him. When he is gone, I will continue to survive in his children.'

Maryam did not ask any more questions. The rumour went around the barracks that the woman in the death cell was very brave and pious; she had received a revelation that she would live even after she was hanged.

Narjis noticed that whenever the lady warden visited her, she came with her gaze lowered, the jail superintendent would always be in a hurry to leave her cell, and every morning and evening, when she was let out of her cell, a sudden hush would descend all around. The noisy, quarrelling women would suddenly quieten down and stare at her from behind the bars.

The last meal was served with the utmost respect. The Last Supper – she was reminded of the painting and the great artist.

Mehdi was delighted with the food. 'Ammi, the food is delicious today,' he cried gleefully and put his arms around his mother's neck.

'Yes, darling, you are right.' Narjis gave him a bite to eat and lowered her gaze in order to hide the tears trembling on her lashes.

Night fell. Mehdi began to doze. But Narjis wanted to talk to him to her heart's content. She wanted to hear his voice as long as she could. She wanted to keep him awake for a while because when they came to take her before daybreak, he would be lost in sweet slumber. Narjis kept looking at his radiant eyes and his handsome forehead. They were Haseen's eyes and Haseen's forehead. His body exuded Haseen's fragrance – the fragrance of beauty, the fragrance of life, the fragrance of hope.

'Haseen, now that you are nowhere, is it possible that you are still alive somewhere? Between heaven and earth?'

Her blood threatened to burst out of her veins. She clutched Mehdi tightly. 'I am very sleepy, Ammi,' Mehdi pleaded.

'My darling, you can sleep in a moment. Talk to me some more.' Her voice began to quiver. 'Tomorrow morning, Mama will take you home with him. He will tell you stories and take you to the market. You will go with him, won't you?'

'Really, Ammi? Will you come with us, too?' Mehdi sat up, wide awake.

'I will not go with you.'

'Then, will you stay in this house?'

'No, I shall go looking for butterflies for you.'

Footsteps echoed in the passage. Narjis raised her head and saw Warden Maryam holding the prison bars, watching them.

'Ammi will be looking for butterflies tomorrow,' Mehdi told Maryam gleefully.

He had never seen butterflies, but Ammi had told him many stories about them.

'Yes, my prince, talk to your mother to your heart's content and give her many kisses.' Maryam's voice began to falter and she hastily turned away.

'But you will return by evening, won't you?'

'No, Mehdi, butterflies fly very fast and I shall be gone very far.'

'But which butterfly will you be looking for?'

Narjis paused a moment.

'The butterfly of freedom, my darling.'

'What colour is that butterfly?'

'It has the seven colours of a rainbow.'

'What is a rainbow?'

'The next time when it rains, you must ask Mama to show you a rainbow.'

'Then I shall look for rainbow-coloured butterflies, too.'

'No, my darling, the rainbow-coloured butterflies will come to you on their own. The reason why I must go looking for them is to save you from travelling so far.'

Narjis's body began to tremble. As though in a frenzy, she began to kiss Mehdi's smooth unblemished neck.

It was more than a week since she had allowed herself to cry. When Mehdi fell asleep, she picked him up and lay him on her chest. It was in Mehdi, in his existence, in his very being as it were, that the flower of hope was being nourished. It was this hope that had instilled in her boundless courage and had given birth to the revelation that she would continue to live too. From the barracks nearby came the murmuring sound of readings from the

Quran and prayers. Some woman was reciting the Surah Rahman in a melodious voice. They all knew that Bibi was going away today and this was their way of bidding her farewell. A thought pierced her heart. She realized that her brother would be sitting in the dust near the main gate of the prison. An M.Sc. in statistics would not have prepared him in any way for this day when he sat counting the moments of his sister's life, so completely alone.

Faces began to whirl before her eyes. Kind and unkind faces, strange and familiar voices. Narjis suddenly felt a surge of love for the voices that had sacrificed their sleep to make her last journey easy. For a whole week, these voices had given her companionship, though they had not been able to understand her one bit. They knew nothing about her. When the time for the appeal for mercy had expired, a message had come that the superintendent and deputy jail superintendent would arrive to transfer her to the death cell. There had been silence all around. As Mehdi and she left the barrack, she had seen some women wipe their tears quietly and lower their heads. These were women who cursed each other on the smallest pretext and tore each other's clothes violently. Often, the matron and the warden had to use a whip to separate them.

Narjis's eyes blinked with sleep. Her heart ached. Mehdi's heart was beating alongside hers. The continuous beating of that little heart was her victory over death. She would continue to live after death. But what exactly, she wondered, was the soul, and if it did exist, where did it reside after it left the body?

Where was Haseen? Nowhere.

Everything had been destroyed. What was the meaning of mortality? She knew it only in a literal sense, but soon she would be able to experience it in its totality.

'Bibi.' Maryam came close to the bars and called in a low voice.

'Yes, Maryam?'

'Lay prince on the bed, Bibi. Those people are coming.' Maryam's voice was trembling with emotion.

For a moment, Narjis felt the ground shake. Then taking hold of herself, she turned over, gently moved Mehdi, who was clinging to her, and laid him on the bed.

'He won't even remember my face in a few days. For him, I shall become a mere name, a mere thought.'

'Forgive us all our wrongs, Bibi, this is how we earn our bread. The belly is ruthless.'

Maryam began to sob. Narjis got up from her bed and reaching out through the bars, she touched Maryam's shoulders. Words were ineffectual. When the sound of heavy footsteps drew near, Narjis patted Maryam's shoulders. Maryam looked at Narjis, her eyes brimming with tears. Wiping her eyes with her white cotton dupatta, she stood at attention. Then she turned the key in the lock and opened the door as gently as she could.

The door screeched as the jail superintendent pushed it open.

'Sahib ji, the child is asleep,' Maryam tried to remind them with utmost respect.

'Shut up...it's none of your business,' the superintendent scolded her.

'Sir, I request you not to talk so loudly.'

The young magistrate cast an eye on the sleeping Mehdi and wiped the perspiration from his forehead. The superintendent frowned. What did these new officers think of themselves? Then, returning to the matter at hand, he identified Narjis and, unfolding a paper, read out a statement in an official but lowered voice.

The statement began with Bismillah and ended by pointing out that the noose should be placed around the neck of the accused and pulled till she died. The medical officer came forward to check Narjis's pulse. She listened to her heartbeat, and then slowly shook her head.

The deputy superintendent asked her to sign some papers. The young magistrate verified the signatures and the superintendent left the cell. The deputy superintendent signalled to Maryam. She appeared, her face bereft of colour. She tied Narjis's hands behind her back with a leather strap. Narjis felt the trembling softness of Maryam's fingers. She knew she was not alone. There were a lot of people outside. The barracks were guarded by men with rifles. A band of wardens would be at the front gate. They must have loaded their rifles with ten bullets each, and beside them, Bhaiyya would be sitting in the dust. Mehdi's face hovered before her eyes. Her eyes were fixed on him. At a signal from the matron,

Maryam took hold of her arm. 'Come, Bibi.' She took one step and then turned back to look at Mehdi. He was restless in his sleep and sobbing. Perhaps he was in the midst of a frightening nightmare. Something clutched at Narjis's heart. She held back the tears that came to her eyes. She was standing before those people who had attempted to defeat her and others like her, and she had not given in to them yet. Why should she, in these last moments, let them taste victory?

The young magistrate's eyes followed her gaze.

'Where will the child stay?' he asked the matron.

Narjis's heart skipped a beat. What a terrible test she had put before her brother.

The magistrate frowned. He stared hard at Narjis and then called the warden who was standing in the corridor.

'Yes, sahib?' The warden came in.

'Pick up the child carefully.'

'Sahib ji, can I pick him up?' Maryam's voice pleaded.

'Okay, pick him up and carry him along with Bibi.'

'But this is against the jail manual,' the deputy magistrate intervened.

'To hell with the jail manual!' the young magistrate said and quickly left the room.

Maryam picked up Mehdi and hugged him. He stopped sobbing and fell into a deep slumber. With the deputy superintendent leading the way, the group started its journey.

Two guards walked in the front and two at the rear. Narjis was in the middle. On her right was Maryam, and on her left, the other warden. Narjis continued to gaze at Mehdi as she walked.

Outside, the moment before that May night turned into dawn was filled with a pleasant coolness. In the light of the waning moon, she could see the scaffold, the steps.

Death was another name for descending into the underworld. Why did one need to climb stairs to descend into this underworld?

The executioner became visible. How happy his children would be: their father would get an execution allowance today. Ten rupees – ten rupees were a lot. So many things could be bought with this money. Narjis's mind was wandering. But her feet were not trembling. She stopped suddenly.

'Maryam.' Her voice struck the silence like lightning.

'What is it that you want, Bibi?'

Warden Maryam's voice sounded hoarse and tearful. Narjis gestured to Maryam to come closer. Maryam stooped before her. Her hands, tied behind her back, tried to touch Mehdi and then became still. Mehdi was smiling in his sleep; perhaps he was playing with the fairies. Narjis gazed with misty eyes and then gently kissed his forehead and his cheeks; life was bidding adieu to life.

She began to climb the stairs. When she reached the scaffold, the executioner bent before her and began to tie her feet with a strap. Narjis cast a glance at the fading scene, then stored that away too. Her eyes were closed and the scene was inside her. She knew that the moon was waning, the morning star disappearing, and Mehdi was playing with the fairies. Soon it would be time for the sun to appear. And the time had come – to obey the order that began with the blessed name of Allah.

Translated from the Urdu by SAMI RAFIQ

Leaves

Khaleda Hussain

Was it chance? Or coincidence?

Countless scattered or randomly placed dots may suddenly come together to assume a meaningful shape, word or expression. We look at it, read it, and feel amazed. As if the jumbled pieces of a puzzle have managed, one at a time, to reach their proper places without any planning or organization. And we exclaim in wonder – so this was what it all meant!

This is exactly how I felt when I bumped into Malik. Another thing that I knew then was that a person's life is made up of three parts. Man searches for people and things in one, loses them in the second, and reclaims them in the third. Not for nothing have wise men divided life into the three stages of morning, afternoon and evening.

But such things cannot be calculated so simply. Who's going to decide when the morning ends and afternoon begins, or when evening sets in? The morning itself stretches endlessly for some people. The afternoons of some get extended, while others live on in endless evening.

All this crossed my mind as I sat in my small, beat-up car waiting for Qasim at the school gates. I noticed that the silver grey Charade had once again, like it did everyday, parked itself in front. A man whose hair was the same silver grey as the car's emerged from it, and was soon engrossed in conversation with the watchman. There were still ten minutes to go for school to be over, but he must have to go somewhere soon, for he wanted to take the girl away a little early, which was a nearly impossible task in that school. The watchman said something to him and then pointed towards the principal's office. The man looked at his watch, then stood lounging, his weight mostly on one leg, near the tree which had innumerable blood-red flowers hanging from it like lanterns. I had never been able to figure out whether the flowers had blossomed or would bloom just a little more. A strange feeling of uneasiness would overcome me on seeing them. At one point, I had thought of getting a sapling from the nursery to plant in my home, but I changed my mind. One can hardly have a conversation with flowers you can't be sure have bloomed. I was reminded of an ancient tea-set, the pure white china patterned with purple and yellow flowers; the cups and plates had 'Made in Japan' printed at their base. Not a single flower could achieve fullness, for they had all been cleverly left incomplete, though there was no apparent impediment or barrier to their completion. This half-done work never failed to irk me and I would turn the cups and saucers in every direction, hoping that the flowers would reveal their complete form from some angle, but to no avail. A similar restlessness would arise in me on seeing that tree.

At that moment, I saw the grey-haired man walking pensively towards me. He probably wanted to say something about the children. He stopped near the rolled down window of my car. 'Excuse me.' He cleared his throat. 'Are you Rahela?' I nearly jumped up from my seat. 'Why?' I blurted out. How could anyone know me by my name? How strange. I was only Mrs Nasir now, or Roshan's mother, or Qasim's grandmother.

'Yes, and you?' Now I looked at him closely.

'Malik, Malik Salim.'

Malik Salim! A sudden sense of suffocation enveloped my chest.

'Malik Salim…after so long!' I opened the door of the car and stepped out.

'I have been observing you for quite some time. And Qasim and Bisma are in the same class – Lotus.'

In college we had read Tennyson's long poem 'The Lotus Eaters'. The lotus is the flower of dreams and tranquillity, and it blooms in water. The hardworking people in this poem eat the lotus, and drown themselves in a magical state of comfort and tranquillity. Doubtless, doubtless sleep is better than travail. But I hadn't yet gained control over my racing pulse. Salim had changed so much, except for the scar on his cheekbone, below his left eye. We used to play tipcat and seven stones in the scorching afternoons on deserted roads, and hold high-jump contests on Salim's spacious lawn. Their house was located on the right side of a lane that opened on to the main road. A black Ford would be parked in their porch. Two uniformed men stood guard at the gate, guns in hand.

How thin and dark Salim had been then, his thin legs dangling below his shorts. His black shoes were always properly polished. He seemed to suffer from a perpetual cold and his hair had already started to grey on the sides.

He had begun to wear glasses too. His lips would droop because he breathed from his mouth due to a perpetually blocked nose. Often he would only hear something if it was repeated twice. But now Salim Malik stood before me, tall and handsome.

'Where are you now and what happened to all the rest of them?' The watchman had brought the children to us by now.

'This is Bisma, my daughter's daughter.' He stroked Bisma's thick golden hair. 'I'm Professor of Surgery at the Teaching Hospital here.'

Oh my God! I was deeply impressed. As usual my confidence level plummeted. *Unaccomplished, you never did accomplish anything.* The verse echoed in my mind. I saw people leave with their children one by one. The rush of traffic on the road thinned out.

'And you…what have you been doing…what are you doing?' He had chosen to be informal suddenly. I opened the door to seat Qasim inside the car. 'Me? I just spent my time teaching girls…'

I left the sentence unfinished. I realized I had nothing to say about myself. Even my beat-up car seemed an embarrassment at that moment. I suddenly thought of Nasir; what would he think if he knew that I was sharing memories with a childhood friend?

The next day, I readied myself for school a little earlier than usual but not in the usual careless manner. I discarded the chador I always wrapped around myself like a shield before going out. I took from my wardrobe a presentable shalwar suit. The clothes had been lying unused for so long that they had begun to smell musty. Antiquity and oblivion have a smell of their own. I moved the hangers one by one. A variety of dresses, hanging there quietly for so long. On looking closely, I could see life stirring in them. These weren't clothes; they were living beings that had been forsaken to solitude and darkness. I took out a dress, and placing it against myself, looked into the mirror.

'Where are you going?' Nasir asked, peering over his spectacles.

'To fetch Qasim.'

'Oh, there's still plenty of time.'

'I know.' I removed the clothes from the hanger and flung them over my arm.

'There's a child, Bisma… She's in Qasim's class.'

'So…? There must be many children.'

'So, she is the granddaughter of someone who…our houses were side by side in my childhood.'

'There are many houses side by side.' Nasir stared at the computer screen.

'Yes, that's also true. But all houses are not like this one.' I thought about it all the way to the school. You enter the house after climbing two or three steps. Here is the courtyard, the right corner of which has a staircase leading to the upper storey. Facing you are the doors to two huge rooms. There was no concept of bedrooms then; there were just rooms with four-poster beds in them. The huge bedsteads with painted legs, woven with tape, are covered with rough cotton damask sheets with large black and white squares. The huge pillar-shaped bolsters have machine-embroidered covers. The tables are covered with crochet tablecloths.

In the winter, outsized woven jute charpoys would be put out in the sun. The elder Malik sahib would sit gurgling his hookah, wearing a snow-white wrap-around sarong-like cloth, kurta and short turban. On the other, the elder Malkani would sit with the wheat spread out on a durrie, winnowing the grain. In spite of her rural, land-owning background, she had sent her only son to Cambridge. Shuja'at was tall, sturdy and dark complexioned, and had strong features. He was a Superintendent of Police. He could often be seen on the streets of the city riding a sleek, lively, muscular horse, ambling along majestically. Occasionally, in the course of his morning ride, he would bring his horse to our house too. The horse would stop somewhere near the outer veranda. Shuja'at Malik would talk to Abba without dismounting. The horse's nostrils would blow hot air and sometimes, in an entirely irresponsible gesture, it would relieve itself. Shuja'at Malik would utter a reprimand or two in a highly refined sort of English and set off waving his whip. Behind him, the scent of his expensive eau de cologne would mingle with the animal smell of the horse.

Salim's mother was a tall, well-built village woman with an urban air who could sometimes be seen wearing a loose petticoat-like garment and long kurta. Her hair was always slick and oily. She wore a diamond nose-pin in her longish nose and heavy gold bracelets on her arms. She was busy in the kitchen most of the time. Her thick lips seemed extremely dry whenever she spoke, and her feet were perpetually swollen. Uncle Malik's room was in front of her room. It had an inviting dressing table loaded with innumerable lotions, perfumes and creams. I happened to enter his room by mistake one day. Dressed in breeches and long black boots, Uncle Malik stood brushing his hair. He sprayed some freshener into his mouth and sauntered out, humming to himself. Outside, Salim's mother with her swollen feet and oily hair and dry lips sat counting the eggs and chicken that had come from the village, and the entire area was redolent with the smell of curd and ghee.

There comes a big gap in my memory after this. I don't know what happened afterwards. Maybe they were transferred to another city. The house remained empty for a long time and the guards disappeared. But there were many others, apart from Salim. I tried to remember as I applied the brakes at a traffic signal. How did all of them disappear from sight? Who knows, perhaps they wondered where I had vanished. I couldn't help laughing. I had not vanished, not by any means. I was very much here, had been all these years. So much so that my shoulders had started to crackle, and the bones of my feet had become misshapen.

I reached the school well before time, but was surprised to see that he was already there, waiting for me. I couldn't decide whether to remain inside the car or step outside. If

I got out, my twisted feet were certain to be noticed in my insufficient sandals. He was a doctor, after all.

'So what happened to all the others?' he asked without warning. 'All those children…Khurram, Shaista, Shahwar and Yusuf?' I had forgotten even their names, but now I suddenly recalled every single face.

'No idea.'

'You remember him at least, that Ameer Ali.' He looked at me expectantly.

'Ameer Ali? That Syed Ameer Ali?'

'Yes, yes! That Ameer Ali!' He stressed.

I recalled Syed Ameer Ali clearly. He lived in the corner house on the main road. A small, thin, pale boy. He used to insist on being called by his full name. If someone called him Ali or Ameer Ali, he would stop the person mid-sentence: 'My name is Syed Ameer Ali.' At the time, I didn't realize the importance of 'Syed' being attached to one's name. Syed Ameer Ali, that pale, thin boy, was known for doing all kinds of unexpected things. He didn't go to school regularly like the rest of us, nor did studies hold any importance for him. He was the only brother of many sisters and his sisters thought him a genius. This was probably why, while on his way to school, or back – whenever he went that is – he would tear out the pages taught in school and throw them away.

He took our entire group home with him one day. His room was at some distance from the other rooms in his house. All of us were awestruck by the fact that he had a room to himself and that the servants would knock before entering his room. A strange spectacle awaited us when we entered the room. Books lay strewn all over the floor. A blackboard hung on one wall. Long arithmetical calculations with large values in algebraic notations were scribbled all over it. In a corner were strewn parts of a dismantled machine. God alone knew what it was. Torn pieces of greasy cloth lay scattered all over the floor. We gazed, quite astonished and a little scared. Ameer Ali picked up a piece of chalk and started to draw the diagram of a machine furiously, oblivious to our presence in the room. I was the first one to slip away. In any case, elaborate mathematical formulae made me uneasy. *Unaccomplished, you never did accomplish anything.*

'Yes, Syed Ameer Ali.'

'I met him just by chance, just like I met you. He came to me to get a lump in his arm removed. I recognized him only by his name, otherwise he is completely transformed.'

'Oh, I am sure we have all changed.'

I looked at his dignified and handsome face with envy.

'No, by transformation I mean that…' he stopped. 'Actually, he has become senile. Though none of us has reached that age yet, he has certainly changed. Sometimes it seems to me that his mind has become extraordinarily sharp, it is we who regard it as the infirmity of old age. I suppose you know that he disappeared from home many years ago? After a long gap, we came to know that he was in Germany and was teaching at some university there. He won many awards too. Obviously, such useless bits of news are hardly paid any attention to in our part of the world.'

'Yes.' I spoke while looking at the children emerge from the school gates one by one. Yes, I remembered his sisters used to call him Little Einstein although he either flunked or fared miserably in every exam he took.

Bisma and Qasim had reached us by now. He stroked Bisma's beautiful hair as usual. Bisma was an extremely fair, blue-eyed and golden-haired girl. Her lips were so red that it seemed they would drip crimson any moment. She probably had Pathani blood in her veins or...

'Your family?' A highly irrelevant question escaped my lips.

'I lived abroad for a long time. Lena is Irish. She lives abroad most of the time. These days, my daughter is with her mother. I too spend a good portion of the year there. And you? Your hus...?' he left the question unfinished. I chose to ignore the question as I didn't have anything of consequence to tell.

'Is it possible,' he said haltingly, 'is it possible that we look up Syed Ameer Ali on our way home? He lives nearby with his son.'

I sat Qasim on the seat next to me and shut the car door. It wasn't important to see Syed Ameer Ali or visit him. But my days had become so choked with important tasks that there was never any possibility of finding time for the unimportant ones. Besides, a strange desire to see Syed Ameer Ali suddenly gripped me at that moment.

All those things that beckon towards the past suddenly became very attractive. And this was a very interesting situation, with our childhood friend facing senility. I remembered a verse from Mir Taqi Mir.

This madness, oh Mir, is fun
I don't know why people call it an ailment.

His car was leading mine on roads which I traversed morning and evening, and had been traversing for so many years, not knowing that the house with the marble facade, worn-out green gate and autumn-blown leaves on the drive was the home of Syed Ameer Ali.

A dark-complexioned boy riding on a scooty emerged when we rang the bell. He looked at me with surprise but smiled familiarly when he saw Malik.

'Assalam Alaikum, uncle. Bare Abba has been sitting atop the neem tree all morning,' he said as he opened the door.

'Oh, has he eaten anything or not? Come, Rahela.' Malik turned to me. The children were now sitting together in one car. 'This is Rahela, another friend of ours. I told you how our group used to play tipcat and hide-and-seek together and your Bare Abba used to tear off the pages of his books and throw them away. She too was with us at the time.'

'Oh!' He looked at me closely and called out, 'Bare Abba, look who has come! Come down, now!' He went a little ahead of us to a small fall-hit lawn and peered up a huge dense tree in a corner.

'Come on, yaar! This is not fair.' I heard a voice and saw someone climbing gingerly down the thick branches of the tree. The longish face had broadened out. The complexion, though still fair, had a yellowish tinge. White eyebrows, small shapely beard, striped shirt with gray suspender trousers, and gold-rimmed glasses balanced on the tip of his nose: Syed Ameer Ali. He looked at us with the eyes of a stranger. Then an expression of detachment spread over his face as if he couldn't be concerned about who stood in front of him.

'Now this is not fair at all, yaar!' he protested. 'Nothing can ever be moved anywhere. Every action has a reaction. Some formula, some universal rule...Was everything done in one fell swoop? Is it? Let something remain at least which should spontaneously become unruly and go against the universal rule.' He looked at me searchingly.

'When did you come?' he suddenly asked in amazement, and then started off: 'Now look, I'm standing on one foot. Here. I've lifted the hand now. Now the formulae of strength and movement are working. The smallest of actions. All are captive. All are captive.' He kept trying to stand on one foot with both his hands raised, then stood straight with both his arms in place.

'Ameer Ali, how's your arm now? Do your legs still hurt?' Salim asked.

'Look, look, this is also an equation. I'm sick and tired of this slavery. I feel absolutely suffocated. This is not done, yaar. They have trapped us from all sides. Oh, yaar.'

He stretched his arms as he turned towards the sky and called out.

'I think there is something wrong with one of his cardiac arteries or a valve, maybe. Sonny, get your Bare Abba's angiography done.'

'Okay Uncle.' The boy was off, racing his scooty again.

Now Malik turned towards the gate. The children sitting in the back of the car were examining each other's copybooks and pencils. And the long day seemed to spread around us, far and wide. Every being was absorbed in his own existence. Yaar, this won't do, really. I suddenly felt a strange sense of loss. We are all captives. All. Before getting into the car, Malik said, 'I'm going away for a year. I hope you won't turn senile after I'm gone.' He laughed softly.

'And you too,' I said, as I gave Bisma over to him.

The road ahead was choked with dry leaves. A strong gust of wind rose. It carried away some leaves and left some behind.

Translated from the Urdu by BARAN REHMAN

Neither Night Nor Day

Sabyn Javeri-Jillani

I get off the tube at Tooting Broadway. The autumn sun hits my eyes, blinding me temporarily as I emerge from the dark station. I haven't been here in ages, I think to myself, taking in the colourful sight of flying chiffon dupattas and flapping shalwars. The smell of curries and kababs is overpowering and I sway a little, overcome by nostalgia and nausea. A gurgling noise rises from my stomach and I glance up the road towards the Karahi House. It is buzzing with customers of all sorts. White, black, Indian and Pakistani, all grapple together under its tiny roof.

As I get closer, through the glass windows, I see a brown man bent over a plate like a cat, slurping the remains of his curry. Steam from the food has fogged up the windows and I can just about discern the silhouette of a white woman dressed in white lace. She glances nervously at her partner who's standing at the counter waiting to be served. In between the furtive glances, as if she were in a thief's den, she picks at her naan with her fork and knife and takes great, big swigs of water. Children run between the tables while the purdah-covered heads of harassed mothers bob in and out of the curtains in the Family Room, making frantic gestures at them to return. Waiters manoeuvre their way, carrying hot platters of pakoras or bhaji as the British call them, dodging the children and the odd stray cat with expert ease.

'No dogs allowed.' 'Halal only.' 'Bestest Takeaway in Britain.' Garish stickers greet me at the door and a loud bell jangles my ears as I push the door open.

The owner glances up from his till at the sound of the bell, and taking in my dark skin and western attire, scowls at a spot over my shoulder. A waiter passes by, humming a lecherous tune from an Indian film. Another lets out a low whistle and suddenly I feel naked in my jeans and heavy jacket. This is London, I tell myself. A woman can walk in on her own, wearing what she wants, and order what she wants. Surely there are others on their own, I tell myself as I glance around.

There is a fat woman wearing a tight shalwar kurta, her head covered with a chiffon dupatta and a heavy chador draped around her shoulders. A child clings to her on either side and a third is cradled against her shoulder. She is there without a man. Behind me stands a young girl, probably a student. She too is wearing jeans. Her head is covered with a hijab.

'Sister, it is your turn,' she says in her clipped British accent. I step forward in my high-heeled boots, clutching my jacket tightly, and order a biryani to go. The man taking my order takes in my accent, my bindi-less face and asks deliberately, 'Indian?' I shake my head. 'Bangla?' he asks again, a malicious smile playing on his lips. I shake my head again. 'You don't have a British accent,' he remarks slyly as he packs my food. 'I was born in Pakistan,' I say, giving in.

'I see,' he says with a sigh and slips in a flyer, none too discreetly, as he hands me my food.

I step out into the cold sunshine and take in huge gulps of air. My body smells of curry and the smell moves with me as I walk. Grey clouds eclipse the sun, and for a moment, the whole street is engulfed in darkness. It is two o'clock in the afternoon. But here in London, it is neither night nor day.

'The sun here has no warmth,' says a shopkeeper, stroking his long white beard. His eyes are turned towards the heavens and he seems to be talking to no one in particular. There are many like him. Shopkeepers who sit outside their shops on solitary stools, stroking their beards and calling out their wares and making hopeless small talk to passers-by. Unlike in the busy bazaars of Lahore or Karachi, they don't shout out the prices. The price here is to be judged by the appearance of the customer. A pound each for the poor and filthy refugees. Fifty pounds for the blacks who pollute the shops with their very existence. No bargaining, only fixed price for the infidel Indians – let them go to Southall and bargain with their bloodthirsty, snake-in-the-sleeve Sikh brothers. And for the old masters, the goras, whatever you wish to give, Sirji! But nothing here is for free and the whites too have to be categorized: the 'white shirts' who belong to the good clean working class and enjoy the occasional curry, and the 'white trash' who prowl the street looking for a 'Paki' to look him in the eye so they can kick up trouble. Later, you can bleat racism all you want, but can you bring your dead son back to life? No. It is this white trash that the shopkeepers dread the most.

There is another kind the shopkeepers are wary of. They call them 'the enemy within' – the new lot of Pakistani immigrants. The kind with ample money and education, wearing jeans and jackets and sprouting English. The kind that want to assimilate.

I pull out the flyer from the paper bag as I near a trash can. I already know what it's about. The call to Islam, it reads. Sister, embrace the truth! Adorn the hijab! Obviously written by an insecure male, otherwise known as the all-knowing, self-righteous mullah. I hesitate as I put out my hand to bin the paper. My mother's words, as we played on the roof in our house in Karachi, come back to me. 'It is a sin to trash anything with the name of Allah on it.' My hand hovers over the bin. I let out a sigh. Here I am, living in the West, not caring in the least what the community or my family back home think about my life, yet I can't bring myself to trash a piece of paper. I can imagine what will happen over the next few days. Having carefully folded the paper in my pocket, I will keep looking for flowing water to put it in. This is the only honourable way to dispose of anything with God's name written on it. Or so I have been taught to believe. A belief I find hard to discard, like a lot of other small beliefs buried deep inside my heart. Although I quickly shed a heap of other closely held values drilled into me along with the fear of God and His wrath. The sweet taste of wine shoved all talk of *haram* deep into a rarely visited crevice in my subconscious, and the intoxicating abandon I felt dancing to club carma beats made me forget that music is the devil's best friend. Fast food from McDonald's and Burger King quickly replaced halal-only Turkish burgers, just as jeans and kurti soon gave way to shorts and crop tops.

A group of girls wearing black scarves with trendy kurtis pass by, giggling shyly at me. I can't help wondering whether they feel pity for me, or envy.

I must have stood there for a while. A white man, a rarity in this part of London and often called 'foreigner' by locals, approaches me, asking if I am lost. Am I? I blink back. Thinking that I don't speak English, he asks again – slowly – if I have lost my way.

I glance up the street to where a group of young boys are handing out pamphlets and calling out to the public to fight against the Jews. 'Stop the war in Palestine, stop the war in Iraq, stop killing our Muslim brothers.'

'I'm not the one who's lost,' I say and walk on. The man shakes his head and goes back to his stall.

Not a hint of Arab in them, I think as I pass the boys. 'Sister, please make a donation for our Palestinian brothers,' says one boy in a heavy British accent. His wheatish Pakistani complexion, grizzled beard and prayer cap send chills up my spine. He is talking to me with his gaze fixed to the ground.

I don't want to support a war that I feel isn't mine. I want to stay aloof, uninvolved, and think of myself as a first-generation immigrant, holder of a newly printed

British passport, and then as a Muslim, and much later as a woman.

But here in Tooting, surrounded by Punjabi and Urdu expressions, colourful chadors, black hijabs, appetizing smells of curries, and cries of 'Stop the war' mingled with the Mullah's pungent call to prayer from a mosque nearby, I waver.

To steady myself, I tug at the inside left pocket of my coat. This is where I keep my new passport. My entry to the forbidden worlds. Like the flying carpet in the Arabian Nights, this magical booklet can take me anywhere I want to go. It can open closed doors. I am not a 'Paki' anymore. I can write nationality: British on the forms. True, they still ask me, where have you come from? And their accent still baffles me just as my pronunciation causes them to cringe. I don't know how to eat a scone. I don't care for marmite or enjoy a game of Foote. But then, I also don't care much for frying onions, the latest cut in shalwars, or saas bahu soaps on Star Plus.

Life feels like an intersection. East, West, Pakistan, Britain. Paki, Paki-British, British-Paki, British? Maybe that's why the kids on the campus call themselves Muslims instead of choosing one or the other, or both, like me. Sailing in two boats, trying to be both, my mother would say. Or, just sitting on the fence, refusing to choose, I like to think. Why can't I be both, I think as I walk past the Habib Bank, Tooting branch. I stop at the gaudily lit Shabnam Beauty Parlour to have my eyebrows threaded. Having my eyebrows done by the surgeon-like beauty therapist at the salons in Central London is something I still haven't got used to.

Shabnam Beauty Parlour is crammed with women having their hair dyed, babies perched casually on their laps. Giant posters of film stars Reema, Meera and Madhuri beam down at me from the high walls. The air is thick with the smell of Charlie oddly mixed with Billimar agarbati. Songs from the latest Indian films blare from a cassette player somewhere inside a locked cabinet. I dash for a chair being vacated by a young girl with bleached golden hair and blue contact lenses. She wears a red top and a tight pair of jeans. She kisses the owner on both cheeks, pulls on her abaya and leaves the salon chewing bubblegum and talking loudly on her mobile. A round of gossip follows her exit. 'If her brother sees what she has on underneath, he'll beat the daylights out of her,' one woman says. Everyone hushes up as Motiya comes out of the inner room to call the next customer.

I like Motiya. She came from Lahore a few years ago, escaping a brutally violent marriage. Her brother and sister-in-law, who own the parlour and the My Fair Lady sari and fabric shop next door, tried unsuccessfully to get her remarried. Motiya cares for no one, just as she knows that no one really cares about her. 'Why should I don a chador over my face for those bearded idiots?' she would joke as she placed a wax cloth over your calves. 'Did they give a brown turd when my husband was beating me senseless?' she would ask as she pressed the cloth hard. 'Ouch!' you'd scream as she pulled the cloth back, all the time grumbling about the beards who couldn't control their dicks and then blamed the poor woman for enticing them. In fact, her language is so colourful and in-your-face that no man in his right mind would dare invite her to the 'right path'.

'She is possessed, there is no hope for her,' her sister-in-law would lament. 'What to do, we are stuck with her. God tests good people,' she would sigh, while making Motiya work a twelve-hour day without wages.

My biryani gives off a strong smell and as I leave the crammed parlour, now smelling of spice, agarbatti and ammonia, I brace myself for the wrinkling of noses and shrinking away that will follow me on the journey home. People will vacate the seat next to me on the tube, move away from me at the bus stop and glance suspiciously at the bag in my hand. I was once called a 'curry head' when I was a newly-arrived immigrant in Britain. I was also called an FOB except at the time I did not know what it meant and eagerly asked the meaning of the person who said it to me. 'Jesus!' he spat and walked away in disgust.

But before I leave the smells and colours of my childhood behind for the odourless, grey landscape of my present, there is one last thing I have to do.

Mangoes. Every year I make a trip to this part of London for the delicious, mouth-watering delicacy my heart refuses to let go of.

Here is a whole stage of mangoes, delicately placed at right angles to make a giant pyramid. 'Produce of

Pakistan' says a sign proudly placed at the top. For a second, I feel a gleaming pride in belonging to the land that produces a thing of such joy. Abdullah, the mango-shop owner, is deep in conversation with a skinny young man. It is late October and by the man's thin attire and Peshawari chappals, I can tell he is a new arrival, a 'fresh off the boat', probably on a visit visa that will, in all likelihood, stretch to three years in hiding. Or maybe he'll claim asylum, I think as I glance at his needy eyes and pinched face. Like Motiya claimed asylum from her violent husband, it isn't unusual for men to claim asylum from the army, political leaders and sometimes even their own families. The papers are full of it. I sigh, and the man, noticing me behind him, moves to one side.

'Ahh,' says Abdullah, weighing the mangoes on his ancient scale. 'Mangoes and cricket – two things that bring all our people together!'

'Only money brings people together,' says the young man bitterly as he glances at a suited man passing by the shop. Dressed in a dark suit and shiny leather shoes with a Rolex cradling his wrist, the man calls out a greeting to the mango merchant but completely ignores the skinny man.

'You can get away with whatever you want, when you've got money,' he says, glancing sideways in my direction.

'That is true,' says Abdullah as he packs the mangoes with straw and strips of paper inside a cardboard box. 'When you have pounds in your pocket and a flat in

Knightsbridge, no one will call you a 'Paki'. They'll call you 'sir'. Good to have you with us, sir!' He chuckles at his own wit.

The box of mangoes tucked firmly under one arm and the bag of biryani clutched in the other hand, my eyebrows arched in permanent surprise, I step on to the tube heading north. I feel content.

Tooting disappears in a haze of darkness as the tube rushes underground. The train becomes less brown and more white as we go north, and I lean back, flipping through a copy of *Stardust* I purchased at the parlour. I can't wait to get home, kick off my suffocating boots and wriggle out of the tight jeans. I think of my loose, comfortable shalwar kameez, waiting by the bedside. Of switching on B4U and digging into my biryani and mangoes. I glance hurriedly at my watch. There is still time before Jack gets home. Jack is my husband. Jack loves South Asian culture but he isn't too crazy about my curries and my Bollywood movies. I once tried to teach him how to eat a mango. 'Here,' I said. 'Grip the mango with both hands. Turn it around in your palms until it is soft and then tear into the skin at the top. Rip it with your teeth and then let your tongue suck out the flesh.' I sucked on the mango with my eyes closed, feeling something close to ecstasy, oblivious to Jack's disgust, as juice dribbled down my chin and stained his precious Persian carpet.

I took Jack to a Hindi film once. But after three hours of song and dance and running around trees, he asked me to forgive him for any harm he had ever done to me and begged me to stop inflicting such torture on his senses. He prefers Iranian cinema, the kind of real, bitter films where people on the screen spend three miserable hours not doing anything. He loves going to talks and more talks while I hate stepping out in the miserably cold weather to listen to someone else's problems. What do I care about the exploitation of women workers in some God-forsaken African country? He can spend hours reading about Islam while I want to get as far away from the mullahs of my childhood as I can.

This is Jack, who practises yoga, reads Naipaul and Rushdie, but seals his clothes in plastic when I cook a curry, and spreads sheets of plastic on the table when I dig into the juicy flesh of mangoes. Jack, who introduces me as Asian.

Jack doesn't understand my fascination for the ordinary. He can't see why the microwave oven makes my heart go ping. Not because I have never seen one but because now I can buy ready meals to cook in it. Jack doesn't understand my adoration of the royal family, given their history of colonisation. Jack doesn't understand why I don't want to live in my country but bring back all kinds of smells and tastes to recreate the memories I have left behind.

Jack can't compartmentalize me. Just like the people in Tooting can't. I am part of a nameless mongrel humanity with nothing to claim as my own, not even the land I stand on or the roads I left behind. A hybrid without firm beliefs or heroes, neither haunted by a search for the self nor consumed by identity like my predecessors. We come and go. We don't belong to anyone or any one place.

It is time for Jack to return. I throw open the windows to air out the room. I spray the flat with perfume to erase the last traces of my food, brew myself a cuppa and switch the radio station from Sunrise to Capital FM. 'I'm like a bird,' sings Nelly Furtado. 'I don't know where my home is…'

'Where my home is…' As I draw back the curtains, I notice the sky is lit up with stars though it is not yet night. A wan sun peers out from behind thick layers of clouds amidst the faint twinkling of stars. 'Only in London,' I muse, 'can the sun and moon shine together.'

The Breast

Soniah Kamal

The breast is a gigantic wad of fat. Getting rid of both of them will mean getting rid of at least fourteen pounds. Getting rid of one, seven. Seven pounds of shapeless fat sliced off painlessly, while I lie on a table surrounded by people who care for me, who have been paid to care for me.

I'm the first person in my family to have my breast cut off. Unless I go through with this, I won't live. At least, not live well.

'You deserve it,' Aji keeps saying. 'You brought it on yourself.'

I don't like Aji. She'd have brought it on herself too if she had the guts. The tribunal cuts off a man's tongue for blasphemy and his right hand for a first robbery. It believes a chumped penis is a fitting punishment for adultery. Usually I agree with the tribunal. However, it does not seem sane at all to me that feeding someone else's baby should merit my breast being butchered.

Is it my fault that my newborn daughter was wrenched away from me? I barely saw her face. She looked like a shrivelled kumquat, yellow and wrinkly. Her gumless mouth was already sucking at something in the air. Perhaps she was preparing for the moment her little mouth would suckle at my breast, sip at the milk already beginning to seep down my tunic; I imagined so.

It was wrong of me to have imagined it.

'That's when your transgression began,' Aji said. I should have looked at my newborn daughter – no, merely, simply girl – and said, 'Take her, bury her.'

I couldn't.

I had always thought I could.

I have been midwife at many a birth. I have seen the pleasure when a boy is announced, and I have seen the disappointment and pain, although they try to hide it, when a mother hands over the baby girl and says, as the custom goes – 'Take her, bury her.'

I dream of a world in which there are wizards, magic and machines that can tell what sex the child will be born with. Who then would wait for nine months to hear of a girl? Certainly not me! Magic machines would make life much easier. Mothers could then get rid of their daughters well before their birth. Before seeing their faces or hearing little mouths sip sustenance from the empty air.

I thought I was going to have a son. My tummy hung low and was nut-hard. I craved smoked tamarind - another sign of a boy in the offing. Now, I wonder if my cravings were natural or nurtured. Can imagination play havoc with taste buds as well? Can shying away from imagining the worst make it less intolerable?

I have held newborn girls in my arms and passed them to the burial committee with no more thought than what I was going to have for dinner that night.

I did not flinch, my heart would beat steadily and yet, last week, when they took my baby away, my heart began to beat with bewildering wildness and followed them, insisting that it be buried with the child I had carried for nine months and three and a half weeks.

Aji did tell me that my little one was asleep when they laid her down. That she continued to sleep even when the first shovel of grit fell on her face sandwiched between those tiny fists of hers. I like to think that my little girl was defiant. Bold in her uncrying silence. Calmly ignoring the tribunal that was suffocating her to death.

My husband is not speaking to me. He is speaking to the tribunal, though. Telling them that he does not want to remain married to me once I become breast-less. Aji says that the tribunal is trying to convince him that once my breast is chopped off, I will have paid my dues to society. I would have suffered the punishment for breaking the law without any need for extra punishment from him. Aji says that my husband is trying to argue with the logic that one is rendered innocent after suffering punishment.

'She's not innocent by any standards,' Aji shouted. 'Not with a lopsided chest proclaiming otherwise to the world.'

I am not surprised that the tribunal is displeased with him. They argue about what he will do for a wife if they allow him to let go of me. You see, there are no women left in the Reserve. The last one, a Declared Beauty, was doled out to an unanticipated widower. His wife fell into the river. They said that he wasn't able to save her. If you ask me, I think he not only watched her drown, but pushed her in too, in order to get the Declared Beauty. When I decided to report my suspicion to the tribunal, Aji ordered me to hush.

'Try not to be too clever,' she said. 'You know what they do with accusers who are proved wrong. You want your tongue spliced in two?'

'No.' But neither had I wanted my left breast cut off. I wish now that I had accused that man of murdering his wife and risked my tongue being spliced. Now, I've got a few hours left as a whole-chested woman.

As soon as my daughter's face was shown to me, I grabbed hold of Aji's hand.

'Check if it's a boy,' I begged. 'Check if a boy has been born anywhere, even in the next zone.' For the birth of a boy would be able to save my baby girl.

'I've checked.' Aji whipped her hand out of mine. 'It's your fault. It's all your fault.'

Indeed it was my fault that my baby was going to be put to death. Zore had offered well before my delivery.

'Let me,' he'd said, 'impregnate my wife so there's a Life Giver should…'

'There will be no should.'

'Should,' he continued, 'a daughter be born to you.'

I had laughed at Zore. I'd laughed at all the men then. I'd laughed and said, 'I promise you I will give birth to a Life Giver myself.'

Only a boy would jabber out of my womb. My mind was made up. My tummy hung low and was nut-hard. I was craving smoked tamarind.

How could I possibly have known that I would give birth to a girl?

How could I have not prepared in case of one?

I killed my daughter because I did not take the precaution of having someone else give birth to a son. She would have had a partner then and thus an assigned purpose in life. We don't keep girls otherwise. Those in the Reserve are the product of fraternal twin births. The tribunal believes that the female part should not be killed for it could very well hamper the male part. I wish I hadn't laughed at all the men. I wish I had recognized their alliance for what it was. Now my little girl has been buried alive and my left breast is being cut off.

I had just wanted to be suckled, to know what it would feel like to be suckled. To have a gumless rind pull at the hunger in my heart, feed at the nourishment my body was making. I had tasted the salt in my own milk. I wanted a baby to taste it too, and so I tried to feed the first baby I came across in the afternoon when most were blinded by the sunlight.

Aji caught me with the baby at my breast.

'Don't tell them, Aji.'

But already I could see her running hard in the direction of the tribunal. She's a good citizen – Aji, my mother. I should be proud of her for keeping our rules and regulations. In due time, I will either learn to be like her or pretend to be, for otherwise they will put me to death. In due time, I might prefer death.

Five Queen's Street

Sorayya Khan

Rubina loved the garden. She had never lived anywhere with a garden. The first time she walked up the driveway and absorbed all the space around Five Queen's Road, she did not know what to make of what she saw, except that it made her happy. But then, when she allowed herself to study the bedded terraces, the perfumed bushes, and the purple that clung to the walls of what would be her father's library, the idea of filling space with colour and perfume made exquisite sense to her. She too wanted to have a room that was wide open and filled with garden smells and textures. Instead, she settled on skipping through the terraces and painting the flowers – not thousands of little bunches like the perennials outside, but monstrous single ones that filled an entire canvas each. She stored her flowers behind the cupboard for when she would have her own house with a man in it. A man who would allow her to put up things on the walls besides the calligraphic hundred names of God and the wooden panels with brass inlays of Allah that her father constantly received as gifts.

A few hours before Rubina noticed unfamiliar men in the front garden on a school holiday, she brought out the canvases from behind the cupboard and glowed as her friends reacted to her work. They were helping her decide which one to enter for the school's annual art competition. When her friends left, she found herself alone because Yunis had been granted a rare afternoon off. Not that Amir Shah would mind her being alone. An unexpected benefit of sharing the house was that Dina Lal's wife was always on the premises, and although she wasn't particularly friendly, both Dina Lal and Amir Shah expected Rubina to ask Janoo for help if she ever needed anything.

Rubina was in her father's library, sitting at his desk with an open box of pastels that Javaid had secretly purchased for her from the bazaar earlier in the week. She knew that her father wouldn't be home for several hours and this prompted her to risk clearing her father's work from the large desk, replacing it with her drawing materials. As a rule, Rubina found all sorts of excuses to be in the library. She'd told her father that it was the coolest room in summer and the warmest in the winter; it had the most lovely light in the evening and the best view of sunrise in the morning; and the impossibly tall windows made her feel like she was inside and outside at the same time. She never argued with Amir Shah when he came upon her in his library and asked her to leave, but she volunteered reasons for why she wanted to spend time there whenever she could, quietly building arguments inside her head in case he ever returned home and caught her unawares.

Frustrated by her unsuccessful attempts to duplicate the blanket of bougainvillea at the entrance on the large drawing pad she had placed on her father's desk, Rubina's gaze swept the garden, and she noticed that it seemed far less full than before. Bushes that had once been carefully pruned were now uneven and oddly bare, and barren patches had appeared on terraces that were once thick with flowers. Weeks earlier, she'd seen people she didn't recognize cutting branches from bushes that bloomed in September in fabulous reds, before the year's late monsoons arrived. While almost everything else died in Lahore during the long summer of Partition, these bushes remained lush and beautiful because the Englishman's gardeners hadn't yet abandoned their jobs. Daily, as they'd been taught, they soaked the bushes with water from the well. Other times, she watched gardeners cycling down the driveway with barely concealed bouquets of fresh flowers under their chadors. When Rubina rose from her father's desk to push open one of the windows, it occurred to her that the garden might be running out, as if exhausted by the task of bearing such bounty.

Rubina saw four men in the driveway. She climbed on to the sill and strained to recognize them, assuming that the only man with a scythe was one of the few gardeners who still lived on the premises. But the men's faces were almost entirely covered with chadors and Rubina, at fifteen, was struck by how some men were able to carry their shawls like women, expertly draped across their heads and shoulders, and over their mouths. She stared at the men as they neared and it wasn't until one of them passed Amir Shah's library and frightened her with his shout that she dropped to her knees and hid from sight. The men, obviously absorbed by something in the house at the back, didn't see her even though they passed by close enough for her to feel the breeze from their brisk passage, through the open window. She stayed on her knees until their footsteps faded. She heard the hum of Queen's Road traffic, the stops and starts of diesel cars trying to get across town. Above it, she heard the solitary cry of a street vendor who had made it his routine to stand at the entrance and recite a singsong poem explaining why children should buy his ice cream. In the particular way of an adolescent, she momentarily set aside her fear of the unknown men and felt intense anger for the vendor who stood in her driveway every day rattling off silly poems despite the fact that she was too old for his rhymes or his ice cream.

When her fear returned, she stood and rubbed her bony knees. She ran to padlock the hasp and metal staple of the library doors, and rushed through the front house to do the same with the veranda doors. In the living room, she was stopped by sounds on the other side of the barricaded archways. She carefully squeezed between a bookcase lying on its side and an end table piled with a gramophone and records. She stood with her ear against the curtained pane of a French door inside what had once been an elegant doorway. The sounds were no longer muffled and Rubina could distinguish heavy thuds and a few high-pitched shrieks. Janoo was calling for Dina Lal and Rubina realized it was the first time she'd heard the woman address him by name. This made Rubina worry even more about what the men were doing to her. She ran back to the library and kneeling under the ledge of a window, wondered what to do. She closed her eyes and wished that Yunis, more than anyone else, was in the house.

She was so frightened that when the front door rattled, she bumped her head on the window ledge and her eyes filled with tears. Hearing Javaid's voice at the door, she rushed to open it, pulled him in, and in a frantic whisper explained what had happened. Her trembling hands almost dropped the key as she relocked the door behind him and fell back on her knees in her hiding place. A few minutes later, they heard footsteps and the grinding sound of metal against stone. Although she wasn't quite ready to raise her head to look, she imagined the scythe running along the outside of the house and had her initial impression corrected – a gardener would not dull his blade so carelessly. Another man was walking slower than the rest, his footsteps shorter and more shuffling than the others'. Javaid stood still with his back against the locked door and when the men had passed, they both ran to the window. The men walked in a row, the man with the scythe, having run out of wall, mindlessly waving it at his side instead, and another in the middle, slightly behind the rest, walking slower and carrying something over his shoulders. While Rubina strained to see what was hidden in his shawl, an unusual breeze blew and picked up a fold of the roughly woven wool. Underneath was Dina Lal's wife, Janoo, her round face swollen with bruises, her back arched unnaturally over the man's shoulders, her arms bound together with a thick rope bracelet and dangling behind her head. Janoo's eyeballs rolled in her head from side to side as if, Rubina later imagined, in a frantic survey of what she was leaving behind. Forever after, Rubina believed Janoo had looked directly at her and held her gaze. Javaid stood behind her, his hands heavy on her shoulders, while they watched Janoo plead for help by squinting, widening, and eventually closing her big black eyes.

When the men were out of earshot, Rubina jumped up and begged Javaid, 'Do something.' But Javaid did not move. He stood with his feet planted on the Englishman's stone floor and reached for his sister. Rubina pulled away, stumbling towards the door, trying to fit the key into the padlock and leave on her own.

'Stop!' Javaid shouted harshly. 'Think for a moment. Please! We don't want them to return and find you.'

'But they aren't after girls like me!' Rubina insisted, not heeding her brother's words.

'Like you?' Javaid inquired.

'Muslims. They've come to take Hindu girls away, idiot!'

Javaid, who routinely stood first in school exams and won Amir Shah's scant praise because of it, hadn't yet thought of this. But with the bloody events of Partition only a few months behind them, Javaid recognized that his sister might be right. Still, he held on to Rubina with a steel grip until he thought it safe to let her go. When Javaid believed the men had gone far enough, he ran into the street to ask if anyone had seen four men carrying a big bundle over their shoulders. All he learned was that the men and their load had squeezed into a city taxi and made off together.

Rubina stood waiting, her forehead and upper lip wet with perspiration, her wide shalwar accidentally rolled into its cuff, up to her shin.

'You didn't do anything!' Rubina said accusingly when Javaid returned. 'Why didn't you do anything?'

'What could I have done?'

'Stopped them! They took her.'

'There was only one of me and four of them,' Javaid pointed out sensibly.

'You didn't even try. And you're in the boxing team in your school!'

'I didn't want anything to happen to you. We're very lucky they didn't get you.'

'She'll be all right, won't she? They won't kill her, will they? We must report it to the police.'

'Yes,' Javaid answered, deciding to wait for Amir Shah's consent before filing a police report.

'What will you tell Dina Lal?' Rubina asked after a few minutes during which the two of them stood looking at each other, various thoughts racing through their minds.

'What happened,' Javaid said, his calmness belying the confusion and dread he was beginning to feel.

After a pause in which she assessed her brother from head to toe and up again, she shouted, 'You'll tell him we

watched his wife being abducted and we did nothing?'
She stomped into the living room where crooked
bookcases, forgotten music and ugly furniture leaned in
archways, forgetting her art supplies on the desk where
Amir Shah would find them, on returning home a few
hours later.

A Brief Acquaintance

Maniza Naqvi

Ron loved Bosnia. That was what made him so charming.

Presuming that this would make him loveable was his fatal mistake. That's what she had wanted to say, but instead she stuck to a brief speech designed to comfort his family. She talked about Ron's fondness for his family in a voice that to her chagrin sounded apologetic when she spoke of how much Ron had loved Bosnia. He had been killed somewhere along the border of Afghanistan and Pakistan – near Waziristan, his wife had said, before inviting her tearfully to speak at his funeral. His wife had found her visiting card and photograph among his things and called on her as one of Ron's friends from Bosnia, which was at best a dubious credential.

'Butmir – February 1998! Right? Am I right? Mind if I sit down?' Ron had said, the first time they met, in an accent which seemed to be almost a caricature of itself – universally identifiable as American from the southern states, say Texas. He had pulled up a chair before she could reply. Leaning back and pushing his leg against the table between them so that the chair tipped back precariously on its hind legs, he squinted his narrow blue eyes, as though trying to appraise her. 'Am I right, Butmir 1998?'

'No,' she replied coldly. 'Sorry.'

'Huh! For a second there I thought you were someone I met years ago at Butmir, probably on a day just like

this, out there in Ilidza, cold February morning –
raining – sleeting – snowing – muddy – out there on the
military base – right outside a pre-fabricated office. Oh
well. Yeah, looking at you now, I can see you're nothing
like her. This woman I'm talking about was from some
aid agency – liaising with us for some project in a
restricted area.'

Self-consciously, she ran her hand through her long
hair. She noticed Ron watching her. There was a slight,
boyish grin on his face. It embarrassed her. She pushed
her hair back from her face. His eyes followed the
movement of her hand.

'Had to turn her down.' He sighed. 'Told her, no
ma'am, no-can-do. Of course, Ilidza is nothing like it
used to be in the good ol' days. Now it's all fixed up –
cafés going up everywhere – factories and hotels.
Boomtown! In a good way, of course! Boomtown – get
it?' He raised two fingers to touch the brim of an
imaginary cowboy hat, then pointed the fingers at her,
clicked his tongue, and winked.

Looking at him, she thought: Crew cut, big ears, blue
eyes, Sad Sack – dumb, awkward, polite, trying to be
tough. He was so perfectly the part. Thinking back now,
she wondered if he had played it.

It had started to flurry and she had not been in the
best of moods. And then there was the jet lag. She
shivered as a cool gust of air came in from the window
that she had opened just a crack to let in fresh air. The
noon-day azaan had just started up in the mosques, and

so had the church bells. The smoky smell of meat grilling from the nearby kitchen chimneys of cevapicci restaurants came in as well, mixed with the damp spring air. The waiter had turned down the techno pop Bosnian music upon her request and now it pulsated softly in the background. She was on her third trip to Sarajevo, staying in a charming pensione in the heart of the old city, Bascarsija. There would be at least three more trips before she could finish her work, researching for evidence on the environmental and medical consequences of the use of uranium-depleted ammunition by the peacekeeping forces in Bosnia. The ammunition had been stored during the war in Hadizici, in an ammunition depot and a tank repair workshop.

It was Saturday and she was trying to read the second volume of the very large novel that she had picked up at the airport bookstore. He was interrupting her. He had just got off a flight himself.

Ron said, 'Well, that's great. I better get going – let you get cracking on that big ol' book you got there. I need to check in. Get a few shut-eyes.'

Later in the week he was back. She was in the same spot, sifting through her field notes.

Ron sat across from her. He ordered a beer, Sarajevsko Pivo, and an espresso double; she was having cranberry tea. She shut her notebook and put it back in its case, setting it beside her on the floor. Anyone walking into the hotel now would think they were a couple, she thought. It would seem like their usual routine: he was talking about his day; she was listening. He was talking about the property he'd seen earlier in the day.

As he talked, she pictured Ron standing at the edge of some mountain road, taking a puff of his cigarette before pointing with it to a site across the river – some lush green meadow melding into the deeply forested mountain behind it. 'If I had my way I'd buy that piece of property right there – put up a bed-and-breakfast place and stay through the summer. Yup! This place is made for tourism. Clean up the rivers – get rid of the plastic shit floating around in 'em, and put a couple of linkage roads to the coast to Croatia and to Hungary and we're all set!' Ron told her how he had done a tour of duty here – hunting down war criminals, petty smugglers, human traffickers, searching out the committers of military misdemeanors. The image she had of him as she listened to his description of the landscape he had seen that day was charming: a man planning a dream, a Louis L'Amour-like character surveying the frontier, thinking of felling trees, clearing forests, living off the land – somebody else's land – making a fortune, calling it property.

Everyone had their way to disarm, to charm. Hers was to seem like the salt of the earth, pour out her soul through her eyes, even add a waddle to her walk should she sense trouble coming or staring her down an alleyway. Ron's way was to tell vignettes from his boyhood; this she understood much later, after careful study. Endearing stories that were intended to seduce any listener – male or female – into wanting to protect him, wrap their arms around him, take him home, or at the very least smile to themselves and say '*Awwwww*!'

She remembered his hooking line: 'If I hadn't joined the army, I'd have been a criminal.' He talked about himself when he was a teenager. Just before the turning point, when he'd been a juvenile delinquent – the angry son of an angry son.

As Ron told the story, she could imagine him slipping out of his bedroom window – a boy of fifteen with a lithe body and sun-kissed skin – sneaking out from the house at three in the morning and running across the front lawn – he called it a yard. Off he went to be part of the cool bad boys for a night. And on the spur of the moment, just for the heck of it, or because they were running low on gas after a night of driving in their big old chevy gas-guzzler, they decided to rob a gas station. There was a police chase and a car crash. When Ron's dad came to pick him up at the scene of the crash, he lunged for Ron. 'The guy tried to attack me! I swear he was so mad he'd have killed me, I could tell.' Ron's dad had had enough. But the cops got in between. The cop had a gun and so the guy carrying the gun saved Ron from a thrashing from his father that night. Ron hated his dad. He hated him for his drinking and his drunken anger and his drunken violence. One night his dad had got so mad that he put his fist through the kitchen wall. But Ron loved his mom; she was an angel!

Ron kept talking. She listened to him and watched the snowflakes crashing against the windowpane. These

stories, she judged, were the stuff that drove this man —
to countless Bloody Marys in the departure lounges of
countless airports and to countless *Hail Marys* in
monasteries such as the one at Medjugorje. He reached
under the neck of his shirt and pulled out a tiny silver
medallion with the Madonna's image, kissed it and put it
back against his skin. These were the stories and their
variations, she decided, which drove him to places full of
stale smoke and women sitting by themselves in cafés
reading novels.

Ron talked on about his teenage life, inhaling the air
deeply or drawing on his cigarette, squinting, shaking
his head at a memory, hesitating or pausing, saying 'yeah —
that's right,' or 'y'know what I mean' for emphasis or to
get her sympathy. He spoke haltingly: it gave him
authenticity — a certain sexiness. Like those documentary
films made with handheld cameras where the picture was
not always steady, or in the frame, or even in focus. The
military man melted, a young teenager aching to be
rescued emerged, and with that fell her defenses.

He spoke about manual labour in the sun, heat, rain
and the cold — farm boy, construction worker, logger.
And then, of course, boot camp in the military. Tough
guy. His stories explained the muscle and sinew, the deep
honey-toned skin. Saving up enough money and building
a tanned lean muscular body that made the sorority girls
swoon, Ron got to college on the strength of his sports.
He was a natural athlete, track and wrestling. Of course.
She recalled seeing pictures of various American

presidents who had either been quarterbacks on the American football team or on their college wrestling teams. Ron's wrestling coach had been like a father to him – taught him how to centre himself, how to channel his strength and control and use his anger constructively. The coach taught him how to focus on winning. How to watch for and find his opponent's centre of balance and then to throw him off it. How to compete. How to take pride in himself. Ron had married his high school sweetheart. He was a happy guy.

Ron's pride and joy was his house and the garden. The swimming pool that he vacuumed, the lawn that he mowed and manicured, the leaves that he raked and the weeds that he cleared. He talked at length about weeding. She mentioned that weeds were flowers. He laughed at her indulgently and dismissed the notion with a snort. He had built the deck at the back of the house with his own hands, all by himself. She was impressed. She had made a table in carpentry class in grade seven. He called his house property, the land a lot, the garden a yard. Land, lot, property. She wondered when land meant home to Ron. And his faithfulness, his belief in the church. It was endearingly quaint. He told her about his first trip to Medjugorje. She listened to all this and more over dinner and much Montenegrin wine – Dingac and Vranac, and cognac and cigars. Ron chain-smoked and drank steadily. And spoke to her in his gravely, deep voice pickled in smoke and alcohol. His face was lined by the weather, his body deeply tanned, sinewy, wiry, muscular, lean, smelling of smoke and alcohol, and maybe Old Spice, still healthy in spite of all the cigarettes and drinking. Halting in the way he spoke – not glib, not effortless, not like professors or presenters at conferences and in classrooms. Slow, as though thinking each sentence through – a kind of seductive, opposite of eloquence, thoughtful slow. A thought-through sincerity was what Ron had, she decided.

On her next visit, she still hadn't managed to get conclusive answers to the uranium-depleted ammunition and its effects, but she had got together many interviews and much anecdotal evidence. Now she thought that rather than a thesis, she would work on a documentary film, and she was discussing just this with her co-researcher Harris, sitting as usual in her favourite corner of the hotel bar when, much to her pleasant surprise, Ron arrived, grinned at her and sat down.

Ron stretched out his long legs, folded his hands on his chest, ordered a Sarajevsko Pivo and politely asked Harris a bit about himself. Did he live in Sarajevo, or was he from another part of Bosnia? Harris was from Hadizici. Ron nodded his ah-huh, ah-huhs, asked if Harris had a business card, and it seemed just to be polite he asked her for her card as well and having received both, started talking about himself. As she listened in astonishment, Ron proceeded to tell Harris the same anecdotes one by one, in the same order with the same details in exactly the same way that he had told her. And the young man seated next to her, working for a human rights think tank, was as seduced and as touched as she had been. Ron was baring his soul. Ron, she could see, wanted Harris to like him. Love him, even. She was surprised at how hurt she felt by this, this easy intimacy with everyone. It was a silly feeling – this sense of betrayal. But she suddenly had an insight, resentfully, that betrayal only begins with the complete baring of the soul. The way, perhaps, to detect the beginning of betrayal is to recognize the pattern of that particular nakedness.

The last time she ever saw Ron, a few months later, was at the same place. 'Hi Harris, buddy!' Ron said, plunking himself down in an upholstered chair and interrupting the dinner with her colleagues: Harris, Amira and Zoran. This was going to be his last trip to Bosnia, Ron announced. He was going to Iraq and Afghanistan. He looked around at everyone and beamed. 'I've just come back from a few days up at the monastery in Medjugorje. Thought I'd make a pilgrimage.' Her colleagues, mostly from Sarajevo, listened to this with straight faces. She could guess what they were thinking. They had told her in other conversations about the role that the monastery had allegedly played during the war when, from its pulpit, monks and priests had called for the awful violence spreading like an illness in Herzegovina – in Mostar, Glamac, Drvar.

As the evening progressed, Harris told Ron that he had heard about a secret prison for illegal migrants in Croatia. 'Who knows,' Harris said sarcastically, 'maybe now Guantanamo is being sub-contracted to the Balkans and to places like Bulgaria and Romania! What do you think, Ron? Is the business coming to us?' Ron dragged deeply on his cigarette and snuffed it out in the glass ashtray on the table, nodded, and with eyes squinting, looked at Harris and chuckled. 'Search me. Nope. I haven't heard anything. Tell you what? If I hear anything I'll let you know! Deal?' There was an awkward pause in the conversation noticed by everyone, it seemed, except Ron who was happily calling out to the waitress and ordering Sarajevsko Pivo and a menu to order himself dinner.

Through dinner, over begava shorba, mixed green salad, srpska salad, burak, dolma, fried liver, cevapicci and beef steak, Ron regaled Amira and Zoran with his repertoire of stories. She noticed Harris looking on, amused. After dinner, they ordered coffee and more drinks. Ron gathered them all in for a photograph which he took with his tiny digital camera. 'Say seer! Say pivo!' he instructed jovially as the camera flashed. 'Dobra! Hvala! That's just great! Thanks!' he said appreciatively as he checked the photograph on the screen of his tiny digital camera and showed it around. 'Now I got me something to remember ya'll by!' Looking at the picture, she thought she looked radiant; it must be the flash, and the wine of course.

The night moved on and the group turned to talking about literature and poetry. She noticed that Ron was silent. He was bored, she thought. Couldn't possibly be enjoying this discussion on Mak Dizdar or Meso Selimovic. Later, when she thought about it, she didn't know what had got into her, but she got mean. She suggested that each of the party recite their favourite poem. 'Here, I'll go first. I've got one,' she said. Holding the snifter of cognac in one hand, she recited a poem by Stephen Dunn. Then Amira recited one of Dizdar's poems and then, one by one, around the table they went. She saw Ron fidgeting. 'C'mon, Ron,' she said when it was time, 'it's your turn.' Everyone went quiet. 'C'mon, Ron,' she persisted. 'Give us a poem.' Ron tossed back his whiskey, looked her straight in the eye and began in a deep voice:

> *I don't know and I don't care.*
> *We're the best guys out there!*
> *Go Army – hurrah!*
> *Go Army – all the way!*
> *One two-One two*
> *One two-One two!*

Ron sang like he was doing a morning drill at Butmir.

Everyone grinned appreciatively and raised their glasses and coffee cups to Ron. She raised her glass too and nodded defeat. He had trumped her. Ron got up to leave abruptly. 'It's getting late. I need to get going.'

Ron had said goodbye to everyone – shaken everyone's hand in turn, kissed the women on the cheek, and moved towards her. She moved back involuntarily. He said, 'Aw c'mon! I'm saying goodbye here.'

'A handshake will do,' she said stiffly.

He chuckled. 'You have no idea what you're missing.'

'Oh God!' She was only slightly humiliated.

He replied slowly, 'No, not God – just me, Ron.'

The Job Application

Nayyara Rahman

After it appeared for the third time, I started losing sleep over it.

In this blasted age of technology, it isn't every day that a *Typist Wanted* advertisement turns up. I had ignored it twice already. But if I didn't apply now, I would never make it.

I am quite sure I created a world record that day. Never had a resume been typed with such ferocity; never had a courier deliveryman heard such pleading requests for help. And never had a job application reached its destination with such speed.

The following evening, I was cooking when my son ran in, panting.

'There's a phone call!'

'Who is it?'

'An old aunty.'

That didn't really help. My son Haroon was five. Every woman seemed old to him. But the fact that he was excited, and that it was from an 'aunty' should have meant something.

I wiped my hands on my kurta and walked to the dining room.

'Hello?'

'Is this Farzana Ansari?'

It was a windy, expectant voice with far too much room between each syllable. Distinctly upper class, the kind you would expect a socialite to have.

'Yes?'

'I am Shermain Khan, manager at Z. L. & Co. You have applied for a position here?'

I could hear my heart throbbing. 'Jee...I mean yes, yes madam, that's right. I did apply.'

'For the position of typist?'

'Yes.'

'Are you sure you want this job? Because there are a lot more worthy candidates in line.'

'Yes, madam, quite sure. I...is...is...my application all right?'

'You seem a little overqualified for the job, but that actually gives us all the more reason to want to meet you.'

An involuntary 'Oh!' escaped my lips.

'Can you come for an interview on Thursday, at say two-thirty?'

In Karachi, two-thirty is peak business time. But I would do anything for this job. My heart was throbbing. I needed to sit down.

'Umm ...Yes, yes ...'

'Great. I'll talk to you then.' The phone slammed.

I blinked hard, trying to make my eyes trap this beautiful moment forever.

The lady had said 'overqualified'. But she had also said 'all the more reason to meet...', 'interview' and 'Thursday'. It was real!

All those diplomas, all those expensive evening courses at haughty institutes, all those long walks to second-hand bookshops were finally bearing fruit.

I rose slowly and made my way back to the dal in the kitchen. But 'Thursday', 'interview' and 'two-thirty' orbited my thoughts. It was Tuesday. That meant less than two days to make all the arrangements required.

When you're a widow living alone with your five-year-old, there are lots of arrangements to make. That evening, after I'd done the dishes, checked Haroon's homework, ironed his uniform, and put him to bed, I sat down with my own work. First, I took out all my certificates. They might ask for them. I would have them photocopied and laminated tomorrow. Then, I typed a copy of my resume for myself. Eighty words per minute. Not bad.

After that, I took out the clothes I'd wear to the interview.

Less than eight years ago, my mother had sewn a sky-blue nylon shalwar kameez suit for my dowry. It had a long, flowing dupatta with white flowers and a green border. Though it was plain by most standards, I loved it for its simplicity. When my mother-in-law saw it, she laughed and said these were no clothes for a new bride. And so, for months I had remained decked in saffron and gold and love.

I would have forgotten about the blue suit. Except that on the second day of Eid, as I braided my hair, my husband had said, 'Why don't you wear your blue clothes today?' Even my mother-in-law had beamed when she saw me in them.

That was the happiest Eid I ever had, and from that day onwards, the blue suit had become a talisman and an assurance.

I looked at the clothes again. I had lost a lot of weight since my husband's death, and the clothes had become flaccid with age. I could starch them later. But I had to alter them tonight.

On Wednesday, I was still yawning as I dropped Haroon to school in a rickshaw, but I went to work anyway. For every hour of absence, I lost twenty rupees. Why risk it?

Thankfully, though, it was a slow day, so I was able to slip out during the lunch break. I took a rickshaw to the photocopy shop and quickly took out the certificates. 'Bhai, do it quickly please.'

Secretarial Diploma: Haroon was only two months old. Conversational English Certificate: my father had developed bronchitis mid-way through the course. Typing Certificate: I had burnt my hand while ironing. Diploma in Computer Basics: I had paid the first rent on the house. Zing, zing, zing. The computer delivered powdered copies of my past.

A forced and helpless past.

I couldn't leave the shop soon enough. I checked a clock in a store window. Thirty-five minutes to go. 'Bhai, turn into that lane, please.' The rickshaw driver turned left. The bell had just rung in Haroon's school, and shiny, chatty faces poured out. I spotted Haroon. He waved and ran to the rickshaw. I took his bag and said, 'Look what I have for you!' His eyes lit up when he saw the slim paper package.

'Chicken Roll!'

He dug in immediately, and I felt my heart melt. He would never have received this roadside treat if I had had the time to make his lunch that morning, like I did everyday.

Haroon ate, and my mind wandered. Though it only distributed garments, Z. L. & Co. paid well – six thousand a month, according to the advertisement. That was two thousand rupees more than I was making now. Haroon's school charged eight hundred a month. But the missionary school, which was English medium and had much better standards, charged one thousand four hundred a month. I wanted him to study there. If Z. L. & Co. could arrange for a conveyance allowance, things might work out quite well.

The rickshaw driver dropped us back to my workplace, just three minutes short of a penalty. While Haroon took out his homework, I resumed typing. A little later, when my boss left, I took the liberty of calling up Z. L. & Co. What I needed to know, I said, were directions to the office. 'Oh, it's behind Rakha Hospital,' said an airy, cheerful voice at the other end. 'Are there any other landmarks?' 'Oh, you'll find it.' Again, too much room between the syllables. The line went dead.

Despite noting down the address and the phone number, I was a little uneasy about reaching Z. L. & Co. All I knew was that it was behind Rakha Hospital, in

Bath Island, one of the posh areas in the city. That's why I set out two hours early the next day.

Getting a bus to Bath Island was easy enough. The drive was all right too, except for two little girls who kept pointing to the birthmark on my cheek. After a while, it got so tiresome I was willing to hand it over to them.

'Baath Eyelaind walay! Baath Eyelaind walay! Baath Eyelaind! Baath Eyelaind!' chanted the bus conductor. I rose and quickly disembarked.

It was only then that I realized the bus driver had dropped me a good three minutes before my stop. That's what you get for trusting public transport! So there I was, in my high heels and stiff starched clothes, walking to Rakha Hospital. Click click click click. Sand filled my sandals. The sun blinked cruelly. Plush houses, well over two stories high, loomed around me. How I envied the people inside them, sipping cold drinks in their air-conditioned rooms! If things worked out at Z. L. & Co., maybe Haroon and I would be amongst them one day.

Click click click click. Rakha Hospital at last. But wait. There was a problem. From where I stood, I could see seven lanes stretched out behind the hospital. I approached a young traffic scout. 'Can you tell me the way to this place?' I said, handing him the address. He studied it silently for a moment, then looked up and said, 'I'm not sure, but you might want to try that lane.'

I thanked him and walked on. The reason my sandals looked almost new was that I only wore them on Eid or at weddings. My feet weren't used to the leathered formality, and were already stiffening with pain. I ignored it and walked ahead.

Magnificence, it seemed, expected to be acknowledged in this neighbourhood. There was something foreign and royal about everything, even the phone booth. As I looked at the arches, the fresh paint, the sloping rooftops and the spacious balconies, I felt as if time had left me, and people like me, behind. So much would have to happen before my neck could stop craning to look. But of course, I had to look.

There were tall buildings on both sides of the lane, but none of them housed the office I was looking for.

When I reached an official-looking gray gate, I thought I was there. The number matched too. I peered in through the open gate. There were swings and a kennel. No, it was not Z. L. & Co.

I was about to turn when my eyes met the owner's. He was washing his car.

'Are you looking for someone?'

He was a short, tubby man with curly hair and a moustache. He walked over and I handed him the address slip. 'You won't find this here,' he said, with a click of his tongue.

My heart sank. 'Then?'

'Maybe that one,' he said, pointing right.

'Thank you, sir, thank you.'

He smiled and waved. 'I hope you find it.'

I entered the lane and walked some more. Fruitlessly, as I would soon find out. My mouth felt like cardboard and I was quite tempted to give up the search and go home. But then the bus fare would go waste. All that effort of taking work home so I could leave the office early today would have been wasted. I thought of my mother, who would have picked up Haroon from school today.

Z. L. & Co. promised a tomorrow, a tomorrow that might not come after today. I crossed sides and entered a lane. My clothes sagged with sweat, but I was grateful for the dampness. I still did not seem to be having any luck with finding the office. Perhaps I should ask someone again.

I saw a man step out of a Honda Civic. He was tall, well dressed and rather good-looking. I was sure this man would help me.

'Excuse me?'

'What is it?'

Was that a snarl?

'I…I …was wondering if…if you could help me with…with…this…address.' I held out the paper to him.

He pretended not to hear me. When I repeated myself, he snatched the paper and stared at it for a long time. When he finally spoke, it was to let out another bark.

'Do I look like a directory to you? Or is it suddenly my duty to serve every second-rate clerk in this country?'

He walked away, and I hoped someone would puncture the tires of his precious Honda.

I also hoped that an oasis would spring up soon, because there were thorns in my throat and I could no longer feel the inside of my mouth. Nevertheless, I kept walking. It was five minutes to two. I'd been walking for almost an hour. Click click click click. The concrete underneath my feet echoed in my skull. The sun shone in all its brightness, bullying every creature out of the sky. Even crows, despite all their obstinacy, kept away.

Perhaps I could get a second-hand car. Perhaps, if I saved for a few months and took a loan... Banks were kind that way nowadays. With six thousand a month, it just might be possible.

When blades started scraping the inside of my throat, I decided to stop. There was a public tap about five feet away. The knob was rusty and a little green, but it was the Indus as far as I was concerned. I almost hopped forward, my heels for once proving helpful. A silver cup on a chain dangled on one side. I grabbed it, and my fingers tightened around the knob. The oasis at last! I smiled and clutched the knob, my fingers gripping the steel.

But what was this? It wouldn't move! I tried harder, my hands twisting fiercely, my cheeks contorting with the torque. But the metal smirked at me, its smirk magnified a thousand times in the winking sunlight. I tried again and again, my voiceless throat urging me on. Please, it pleaded. Please. Just one glass, that's all I ask.

But the sheer impossibility of it! In the end, it was my exhaustion and not my will, which told me I would not get water from the tap. I almost flung my sandals at the damn thing.

I swallowed some spit, and glanced at my watch – it was two fifteen! Thirst and fatigue were quickly shoved aside as panic gripped me. Like a blind child, I started wandering through the lane, desperately trying to grope my way forward.

I don't know where I went from there, but a little later I found myself in front of a gray gate. The address matched! And I still had four minutes to go! I rang the bell. It wasn't long before I heard footsteps, and the door was unbolted. A heavyset woman with blond hair and a big smile stood before me. A long olive dress with yellow spots adorned her frame.

'Is this Z. L. & Co., madam?'

Still smiling, she said, 'The gate for Z. L. & Co. is at the back.'

'Thank you.'

She smiled and nodded.

I silently blessed the man who had brought such a saintly creature to Pakistan.

I hurried. Two minutes to go and I was there.

But what a shock! There was no signboard, nor a company logo. The building itself was a cubed pigeonhole, and I wondered how it had earned the endorsement of some of the city's most famous names. I hurried inside.

The receptionist, an icy, unsmiling sort, guided me to the main office. It was a while before someone discovered my presence. One of the girls looked up and said, 'Are you here for the typist's vacancy?'

'That's right.'

'Well, you'll have to wait. Shermain is having lunch.'

For someone who worked in this box, she sure gave herself a lot of airs.

I'd try to be even more punctual next time.

It was exactly two-thirty, and I needed to check on Haroon. I wondered if they would let me use their phone. I hoped they wouldn't feel I was imposing. A request formed on my lips, but buried itself. Despite the heat outside, there was an icy coldness inside the office.

So I changed my mind. Instead, I rechecked my documents, tried to fix my hair as best as I could, and waited. Meanwhile, the girls around me chatted.

'I'm planning to throw a wedding anniversary bash for my parents,' said one with short hair and an even shorter kurta.

'Oooh…How sweet! When is it?' I got a glimpse of bleached hair and plump cheeks.

How ironic that all of them should have the same stretched out, whimsical accents, and the same stretched out, whimsical things to talk about. As the conversation moved on to caterers and photographers, I lost interest.

The four girls in that room were dressed casually, but I could tell their clothes had cost a lot more than my best 'going out' ones. They held their cell phones with dainty hands. I could imagine the manicurist at work on them. Fingernails painted fiery red; beautiful ruthless nails. Faces scrubbed a shiny pink; beautiful ruthless faces. Their voices bounced with every expletive, and despite their obvious youth, I could tell their faces were not unacquainted with beauty parlours.

I wondered if Haroon had had lunch.

'...Zarrain is definitely the best among florists, though you might want to try...'

I wondered how many of these girls had a university degree.

'Farzana Ansari?'

I looked up.

'Mrs Khan will see you now.'

I clutched my folder and went inside.

Shermain Khan was bent over a fruit; a peach, I think. I'd been standing for two minutes before she realized she had company.

'Oh...please sit down.'

'Uhmm...Farheena, isn't it?'

'Uhh...Farzana, madam.'

'Oh. It's just that there have been so many applications, I've rather lost track. Would you have a resume on you?'

I handed it over.

Shermain Khan had the kind of face that had never been beautiful, but had always been made up. She was about forty, but her hair was thick and black, and fell in a sheet down to her waist. I couldn't help noticing that its length was distinctly unaccompanied by the shine that is a mark of every eastern woman's silken mane. Her lips clamped a little as she went through my resume.

'Uhmm…Farheena, there seems to have been an oversight on your part.'

I felt my breath catch. My pupils dilated.

'Farzeena, you never told us you lived in Dastagir. Do you know that all the girls here are from this area? The worst we've got so far is a secretary from Bahadurabad. And she's only working as a hobby. She doesn't really need the money.'

'But madam, why is Dastagir causing a problem? I promise you that I will be very punctual. I will never miss a day of work. I have references. See, please see.'

At this, Mrs Shermain Khan smiled a little.

'Oh, I know that. That's not the problem. You see, the thing is, when people find out that you are from Dastagir, they might get…uncomfortable. We aren't used to working with…with…people of your…background.'

'Madam…madam...please, madam. On the phone you said I had the qualifications and that...'

'Yes, yes, I did. But now, things are different. I didn't know you lived in Dastagir. This creates so many problems. How will you come here every morning from so far away? Tell me!'

'Madam, there's a bus stop near your office. I can take a bus. It's not a problem.'

'And how will you go home? We can get very late here some days, you know. Your parents will be worried about a young girl like you.'

'Jee... madam, I am a widow. There's nobody to worry about me.'

Almost instantly, I saw an eyebrow flicker. For a moment, her face softened. In a different sort of voice, she asked, 'Do you have children?'

'Yes, madam, a son.'

'I see. He must be quite young.'

'He is five, madam.'

'I see.'

She was quiet for a moment, and then she picked up the phone. 'Leena, can you connect me to Safdar Sahab?'

Another pause. And then she spoke again.

'Safdar Sahab. Hi, how are you, sir? How was the trip? How was your daughter's exam? Yes, yes, of course she will do well. She has your genes after all.' There was a burst of tinkling laughter, then she said, 'I'm sorry to be troubling you like this, but the typist I discussed with you is here right now. Will you come to my office? I'm sure she would like to meet you.'

Shermain clapped the phone down.

'Wait a minute. We'll discuss the issue right now.'

'Er...madam. May I ask you something, please?'

She leaned back in her chair and smiled. 'You may.'

'Who is Safdar Sahab?'

She rolled her eyes a little, let out her breath in a sigh, and said, 'The head of the recruitment department. My boss.'

There was a knock, and a man timidly stepped in.

So this was Safdar Sahab.

Perhaps, if you'd been with me, you too would have said that he did not look like the head of recruitment, or the head of anything for that matter. He was a small man, built like a skinny boy, with two twig-like hands creeping out of his shirt sleeves. He held a brown folder in one hand, and a clicker pen in the other.

'Come, come, Safdar Sahab. Please come in.' Shermain rose to greet him.

A quiver, something between an uncertain smile and an uncomfortable frown, appeared on his face. He nodded a little deferentially at Shermain and then turned towards me.

I usually don't have a lot of patience with men like him. They are not used to being their own selves, I have always felt. When they're done with being Mommy's slaves, it's Wifey's turn. If Wifey turns out to be a pushover, the Vixen at Work gets a chance. And it seemed to me that Safdar Sahab had found his Vixen. I felt pity for him.

'Come, Safdar Sahab. Sit.' A wide smile accompanied the effusive gush of words.

A chair's edge received Safdar Sahab's delicate person. And then Shermain Khan began.

'Safdar Sahab, this is one of the applicants for the typist's job. She has been telling me about her life. It might move you to hear about it too.'

When had I told her about my life?

'But before that, Safdar Sahab, please let me request you to let this poor woman have only the morning shift.'

The perplexity on Safdar Sahab's face contorted to full-fledged agony.

'What exactly is the issue here?'

Before I could protest, Shermain Khan ran a hand through her hair, and then the eloquent dribble began to pour out.

'She is a widow, Safdar Sahab. You know how difficult things are for such women. Especially in our society. Farheena over here tells me that her mother is planning to get her remarried, and her chances are very good, as you can tell. Don't you think, Safdar Sahab?'

Safdar Sahab gave a slight smile.

'Some money coming her way would help, of course, but a girl like her – it isn't safe for her to stay out late, especially when she's just passing time before a second marriage. Is it?'

Safdar Sahab managed to get a word in. He tilted his head at me, and said, 'Where did you get your typing diploma from?'

'Index Skills Institute, sir.'

'Ah! You're the one?' Then he said, 'We have three shifts here. It's all right if you can't work the late shift. We can…'

'But sir! She has a child! Who will take care of the poor kid? You know how difficult it is to raise children these days, and with her being a widow…'

Safdar Sahab looked pained again.

'You have a child?' he asked in a choked voice.

'Yes, sir, but I can manage. In fact…'

'Look at that, sir! That's the problem with mothers these days. They don't care enough about their children.

What if they have given birth to children? They are somebody else's problem, right? Your career comes before your child. Is that what you are saying? Farheena, your child needs you! Does this job mean more to you than your son? Do you remember, Safdar Sahab, when your wife was in the hospital? How did you take care of your daughter in those days? Tell her, Safdar Sahab!'

Blood gushed in and out of Safdar Sahab's face, and I could feel the same happening in mine.

'A child is your responsibility, miss,' he finally managed to say.

'But sir, I…!'

'Look, Farheena.' It was a gentle voice. It was Shermain Khan's voice. 'I am not your enemy. We are not against you. You have far too many responsibilities, as it is. We cannot burden you with the problems at Z. L. & Co. It's a demanding job. Just ask Safdar Sahab how hard he works. Ask him.'

She smiled benevolently.

'You need a job that asks less of you. And we,' she said, casting a sidelong glance at Safdar Sahab, 'need someone who has less burdens than you.'

Overqualified? Want to meet you? Thursday? Missionary school? Blue kurta? Eid sandals?

'Madam! Sir! I need this job! Please understand! Please listen to me!'

But they weren't listening. Shermain Khan was already deep in conversation with her boss.

'Remember, sir, I told you about that niece of mine, the one who has just completed her A levels? Her mother tells me that she's really good at typing. And she's a good kid. I will be able to keep an eye on her, if she comes here. She lives in Clifton, only a lane away from my house. And of course, she can always get a certificate.'

A sidelong glance at me.

I called out in one final, desperate attempt. But it was no good. Safdar Sahab was beginning to see the sense of employing a less burdened candidate.

I gathered my things, straightened my kurta and rose. As I slowly walked out of the office, Haroon's smile clouded my eyes, and I thought, not even water. They didn't even offer me water.

A Sandstone Past

Sehba Sarwar

'Hey, check this out!' My sister Huma exclaimed as she dropped on the bed beside me.

I put my book down and turned around to see Huma's name on a black envelope in silver calligraphy. 'Who's it from?' I asked, not really wanting to know. Huma, a couple of years older than me, was part of a group of teenage girls who loved to go swimming at the Sindh Club and hang out at the French Beach. They dressed in tight jeans, wore platform shoes, and flirted with boys. I, on the other hand, had just one best friend, Rovina, and the most exciting thing we ever did was to spend afternoons at Karachi Gymkhana where we dipped greasy fish-fingers in tomato ketchup and speculated about how different the Gymkhana of the eighties must have been from back when Pakistan was not a country and Karachi was just a small fishing village at the edge of the Arabian Sea. The few times that I accompanied Huma to her friends' parties, I invariably got bored. No one else our age seemed to care much about the past, but Rovina and I always felt different.

I opened the card and read – 'Safia Leghari invites you to a birthday dinner. Dress in black and be prepared for anything!' I handed the envelope back to Huma. 'Sounds nice.' Safia was in Huma's class. A slender pale-skinned girl, she wore kajal around her eyes and loved to tell stories about her family in a deep husky voice.

'It's going to be such fun,' Huma said. 'It's her birthday, you know. It will be a sit-down dinner, with tall candlesticks everywhere. Dinner won't be served till after nine and the invitation runs till midnight. Also, it's in the other wing of the house where no one lives, so we won't be bothered by the grownups.'

I knew of Safia's house. Rovina and I had spent many long afternoons brainstorming ways to get inside that ancient building with its inviting open stone staircase and intriguing balconies, but we'd never managed to. Safia lived there with her immediate family, as well as two uncles and their families. Rovina was a Hindu and she claimed that her family had once owned a house right next to Safia's. 'Something strange happened,' she told me. 'No one knows what…but right after Partition, one part of our family left for Bombay, even though they'd said they never would.' Thereafter, Rovina's grandparents sold their sandstone house and moved into an old concrete structure in PECHS. In the seventies, when the town-home craze hit Karachi, her family bought one in Sea View, Clifton. 'That's where I grew up,' Rovina said. 'I never got to enter our old house. And it was torn down when I was ten.'

Rovina's mother could trace their family history five generations back to Sindh and specifically Karachi. Once, I had visited the Hindu temple that was built into a rock cave in Old Clifton along with Rovina, her mother and her sisters. After we climbed down the rocky steps, I saw men and women washing their hands in a trickle of water. I remember her mother telling me, 'These are the same waters in which we have washed our hands and feet for hundreds of years.' Without Rovina and her family, I'd never have known that there was a temple in Old Clifton directly below Playland, where we used to take coin rides, close to Abdullah Shah Ghazi's shrine, or that there were natural waters shared by different communities. When I told my mother about my visit to the temple, Amma said, 'We have water in India also, where Muslims and Hindus wash together. One day, I'll take you to Allahabad.'

After I became friends with Rovina and began spending time at her house, I often wondered what it would feel like to grow up in the same city, the same house, where one's grandfather and great-grandfather were born. Our family, originally from Uttar Pradesh, had settled in Karachi in the fifties. While my Amma and my Dadi loved to recount stories about the homes they had left behind, I could never quite picture my mother's house in Allahabad, where she grew up, close to where the Ganga and Jamna met. And though I was born in Karachi, I knew little about the history of our new city. Partly because the house my parents had bought after Partition was so different from the houses in Rovina's old neighbourhood where Safia lived.

That part of town lay in the heart of old Karachi where buildings were mostly made of yellow sandstone and, even from outside, we could tell that Safia's house carried a sense of history that one rarely felt in Karachi. I had always wanted to go there and learn more, not just about Safia's family but, because of Rovina's stories, also about the Hindu families that had once lived in the neighbourhood. The Hindu Gymkhana, an elegant building that had become decrepit over the years, was also in this part of town, and Rovina and I often discussed possible ways to break past the brambles wrapped around the boundary wall, to explore it one day. But of course, we had never managed that. Safia's house was one of the few large residences in Saddar that were well kept and still in use. And, as far as I knew, Rovina and I were the only sixteen-year-olds interested in Karachi's history and its buildings.

Huma certainly wasn't thinking of Safia's house, Rovina's broken history, or our family's fragmented past. Humming a tune to herself, she opened the cupboard and began searching for black clothes she could wear to the party. I returned to my book, knowing deep down that I should be the one going to Safia's house – I would appreciate it in a way that my sister never would.

At recess the next day, as Rovina and I stood in queue at the school canteen to get tea and samosas, we heard other students chatting about the black envelopes. The girls were discussing make-up and what to wear, while the boys were pretending to be blasé, leaning against the wall and talking about cricket. Later in the day, though, while we waited in front of our school to be picked up, I overheard some boys planning pranks they could play to scare the girls at the party.

'You should try to go to the party,' Rovina said. 'There's a ghost there, you know. I don't know the whole story but there's something mysterious about Safia's family; it's a story that everyone knows but no one talks about. It would be great if you could figure it out, wouldn't it?'

Late in the evening, I was sitting on the window sill behind the dining-room curtains, a book in hand, when I heard Huma's voice. 'Can I go to the party, please Amma? Please?'

My mother clicked her tongue and I could picture her shaking her head. 'No,' she said emphatically. 'Safia lives in the middle of town. What if there's a curfew – how will I pick you up? And there are Rangers everywhere. No one should be out that late, especially not young girls like you.' She clicked her tongue again. 'No grownups around…and who knows what those children will be up to…'

Behind the curtains, I suppressed a smile.

Amma spoke up again. 'Of course, I'd feel a lot better if both of you were going. But…' Her voice trailed away as they left the room.

I slipped out from behind the curtains and raced to the bedroom Huma and I shared. Huma shuffled into the room, chewing on her lip. After she told me what I already knew, I asked her why Amma wouldn't let her go.

'Because…it'll be late. She said she'd allow me to go if you came along.' Her voice was resentful.

I returned to my book and let Huma stew for a while. 'Listen!' I said, thumping the bed so hard that my book jumped. 'How about getting Safia to invite me?'

Huma looked at me doubtfully.

'That is, of course, if you want to go,' I added craftily.

It was after dusk when Amma dropped us off at the end of Safia's long driveway, shaded by swaying old palm trees. Climbing up the open staircase lit by flickering candles, both Huma and I felt like grownups in our black dresses and lipstick. We nudged each other. This was going to be good fun.

Safia's maid, a stooping old woman, greeted us at the entrance. 'Go up the stairs and turn left,' she told us. We walked into the living room. Most of Safia's and Huma's classmates had already arrived. They were lounging on the sofas sipping drinks – some more potent than others – and sharing gossip. The room was dark except for dimmed lamps and candles. Soft whistling music wafted in the background. Safia jumped up to greet us. She wore a flowing black kaftan that made her pale skin glow in the dark. My sister joined some girls in a shadowy corner, while I found a chair in another corner and sat down, staring at my toes, now wishing I had not come, wishing I were not so shy, wishing I didn't feel different from others.

Safia flitted amongst her guests. Pausing beside my sister, she mysteriously whispered, 'There's a ghost in this house! The elevator hasn't worked for a long time, but we hear it rattle and creak at night. I'll tell you guys the story after dinner…'

I wondered why they needed an elevator in a two-story house. After dinner, everyone gathered together to play games. One of the girls, Jamila, placed a twenty-five paisa coin on the table, in the centre, and spread Scrabble letters around it. She then turned off the music and said, 'Okay, everyone, here's how it goes. We all have to put our fingertips on the coin and then close our eyes. We'll wait for a spirit to join us. We'll know it's here when the coin moves. Then, we can ask it any questions we wish. It'll spell out the answer by sliding the letters.'

As many girls as could, placed their fingers on the coin. I held back. There wasn't room for me. Just then, the coin slowly slid across the table. Everyone laughed. Someone shouted, 'Jamila, you're moving it!'

'I'm going to the bathroom,' I mumbled. No one heard me. I stepped out of the room and walked along the balcony lit by oil lamps. It was quiet except for the sound of traffic swishing in from the street. Above the balcony, palm trees rustled and swayed. Moonlight gleamed from behind a row of apartment blocks, the moon itself invisible except for the silver light glistening on rooftops and trees.

I reached a corner and turned. I could no longer hear the voices and laughter from the living room. I wanted to see as much of the house as I could, so that I could take a clear report back to Rovina. In the silence, I heard something creak. I stopped in my tracks and looked around. Somehow, I had entered a long narrow corridor. The lamps and trees were gone. The corridor was cool and white; there were no windows and its whitewashed walls gave off an eerie glow. No wind, no other sounds.

Just my breathing – that's all I could hear. I took three more steps, keeping my palm pressed flat against the wall next to me, hoping that the coolness of the wall would make me feel less hot.

I heard another loud creak, like chains hitting wood. My heart was pounding so hard, it felt as if there was a volcano inside me ready to erupt through the wall of my chest. When I turned around to look, I saw a grilled iron gate blocking off an opening in the wall. And then, a loud rumbling sound burst from within it. Frozen, I crouched low and closed my eyes, hoping I was in a bad dream and would soon wake up. The rumbling got louder and closer. I opened my eyes. A metal chamber had filled the space behind the iron gate where there had been only darkness before. The doors of the metal chamber, the elevator really, opened with much squealing, and a ghostly white face glimmered.

I thought I screamed, but no sound cut the air. The creature inside the elevator was tall, almost seven feet. Or maybe it seemed that way because I was crouched so low, almost hugging the ground. The woman – for now I could see clearly that the face belonged to a woman – used her skeletal fingers to pry open the metal doors. The grill slid back and the woman stepped into the corridor and stood about four feet away from where I lay huddled.

I thought she was looking straight at me, but her deep black eyes seemed to pierce through me to the other side of the wall. She seemed to be searching for something. As she floated closer, the woman's scarlet gharara swept the floor. Her hair was black, parted in the centre and flowing freely around her face, which looked serene, except for her eyes in which there raged a hypnotic wildness. She moved past me, all the way down the corridor, and turned around to walk back to the elevator. I heard more creaking and rumbling. Then the space in the wall closed and the iron grill was shut.

I got up and sped in the opposite direction. Pausing for breath, I stopped and looked around me. I was back in the open balcony and could once again feel the sea breeze and hear the gay laughter from the party. Still in a daze, I touched my cheek and was shocked to find how cold my face was. I crept back into the living room and sneaked into my chair. My absence had gone unnoticed, but I was just in time to hear Safia's story.

'So,' Safia was telling everyone in her husky voice, 'you know there's a ghost in this house, don't you?'

'Tell us,' someone said.

'This house was built by the British in the early 1900s,' Safia said, glad to oblige. 'But then, after Partition, my family – they've always lived in Karachi, you know – bought it from the British and moved in. We lived here back when there was a tram circuiting this part of town from Bunder Road. Sometimes my parents joked that they'd send me to school in the tram.

'But I'm digressing from the story. My great-granduncle lived in this wing of the house. He loved to keep up with everything that was happening in the West.

When elevators were invented, he decided to import one and instal it in the house. Everyone told him not to waste his money, that he didn't really need it, that the technology was still new and not known to be safe. But he would not listen.

'Uncle Farid was in love with a Hindu woman called Sarita and wanted to marry her. Both families – ours as well as hers – were opposed to their union. The story goes that one afternoon, he brought Sarita to this section of the house. She was dressed in a red wedding gharara. He had arranged for a mullah and some witnesses to wait for them downstairs so they could get married in secret. She was going to become a Muslim and change her name to Surayya. Uncle Farid wanted to show off his new elevator to his bride-to-be. "Let's race," he told her. "You take the elevator. I'll take the stairs down. Let's see who reaches first."

'He helped her into the elevator and ran down. But before he could even hit the last step, he heard a crash. The cord holding the elevator had snapped. By the time he and the chowkidar managed to pry open the elevator doors, Sarita was dead. Some people said that Uncle Farid's older brother had somehow found out about the secret marriage and had paid someone to deliberately break the chain. But no one knows the truth really. All this happened right after Partition. Until Sarita died, her family never wanted to leave Karachi. They had lived here even longer than we had. But Sarita was their only daughter and after she passed away, her family got on a

ship to Bombay. They left without anything and never
returned. And Uncle Farid? He left the broken elevator
here as a reminder of his own foolishness.'

'What about the ghost?' I asked, speaking for the
first time that evening.

Safia looked straight at me. 'It's said that the spirit
of Sarita still roams this house searching for my uncle.
He's old, you know, and lives in London. I've seen him
only once. He never married. My maid told me that her
mother and the other servants have heard the elevator
at night. They say they've seen Sarita walking through
the halls all dressed in red. But I've lived here my whole
life and I never have. Who can tell what the truth is?'
Safia stopped and looked around the room at her listening
guests. Then smiling with her lips closed, she asked,
'Want to see the elevator?'

Everyone got up to follow her. Safia turned a few
corners and there we were in the long corridor that I had
rushed out from, just a few minutes ago. But now, with
everyone crowding around, it didn't seem mysterious.

'And this is the famous elevator!' Safia said with a
flourish of her hands.

Everyone crowded around the iron grill. 'Wow!'
someone gasped.

'It's rusty,' a boy said, touching the iron.

One of the boys put his hands on the steel handles
and tried to pull open the grill, but he could not. I turned
away from the crowd and stared down the other end of
the corridor where Sarita's ghost had stood.

Later that night when we were in bed, Huma couldn't stop talking about the party. 'Oh, I loved it when we called the spirits!' She stopped. 'You weren't there. Where did you wander off to?'

I hesitated. 'I went to the bathroom.'

'Whatever,' said Huma. 'You missed a lot of fun. I was sad, though, to hear the story of Sarita. I'd never heard it before. I never knew about Hindus in Karachi...'

I could not sleep for a long time. Tossing and turning restlessly, I wanted to share my story with Rovina as soon as I could. I also knew there was a connection between Rovina's family and Safia's story, and that it would all come together in my mind the next day when I narrated my adventure to her. But right then, in my exhaustion, I couldn't figure out what I wanted to remember and what I wished to forget. Before I fell asleep, I remember wishing that one day Sarita's spirit would find rest and that somehow her family could come home again to Karachi, to the city on the edge of the Arabian Sea, where her ancestors had lived and died.

The Wedding of Sundri

Bina Shah

The day that Sundri was to be married dawned as any other, with the crowing of the rooster in the semi-darkness of dawn, the calling of doves from the nearby forest and the sudden brightening of the sky as the sun struggled to make its ascent. Sundri's mother, Sebhagi, was the first one awake as always, bustling about as she prepared the morning's first meal – sweet flat bread and tea – for the men of the house. Then the men stirred – Mohammad Karim, Sundri's father, and Abdul Karim, her elder brother.

Usually, Sundri was up with her mother at dawn, to help serve breakfast or do any of a hundred chores that awaited her, but today Sebhagi let her sleep for an extra half hour. It was her wedding gift to her only daughter, who would leave their house today to be married to Ghulam Farid, whose family lived in the next village. They were related: Ghulam Farid's father was a first cousin of Mohammad Karim's mother. Ghulam Farid worked as a sharecropper in the nearby zamindar's fields but he aspired to own a petrol pump in town someday. Sundri had been betrothed to him when she was seven years old, the fathers meeting over tea and sweet bread to decide their children's fate. It was decided that she would marry Ghulam Farid when she came of age, and that had happened a month ago. She was all of twelve years; Ghulam Farid was twenty-three.

'It's a good match,' Mohammad Karim had said to his wife when he returned after arranging the marriage.

He was sitting on the charpai outside the house, a vantage point that allowed him to see, but not be seen by, the trucks and buses plying the dusty road. Sebhagi had just handed him a cup of tea. He poured some into the saucer and blew on it to cool it before drinking. She settled down beside him, something that not every wife felt free enough to do in the presence of her husband, but Mohammad Karim was more liberal than most men. He allowed her freedoms that had been unheard of in the village. She could eat at the same time as her husband and sons, she could walk to the nearby houses and spend mornings with the women there, gossiping and chatting with them as they cooked or cleaned, and she could watch anything she wanted on the old television set that Mohammad Karim had mysteriously acquired from somewhere and placed on the table in the middle of the main room in their two-room cottage.

His son objected many times to these allowances. 'Baba, this isn't proper. It's not the way for women to behave. You must tell her. It's a matter of honour, the family's honour.'

'Son, your mother is an honourable woman. Spending time with other women is no threat to me.' Mohammad Karim would pull contentedly on his biri, confident that the matter was settled. But Abdul Karim glowered whenever he thought his mother was taking liberties that were not the privilege of any woman alive on earth.

'Are you sure? Do you know enough about the family?' Sebhagi asked.

Mohammad Karim snorted. 'They're family. What more do we need to know? Haji Ghulam is a good man. Ghulam Farid has studied up to the eighth class – that is quite an accomplishment. Your daughter will be happy with him. And as long as she bears him sons, he will be happy with her.'

Sebhagi said nothing. Her eyes followed a truck laden with bundles of sugarcane as it trundled slowly down the road. Their house was situated closer to the road than the others, and watching the travellers passing to and fro on the busy artery was like having a painting in front of her that changed constantly, from morning to afternoon to evening, never standing still, always flowing with the movement of the rural landscape. Sebhagi could feel the currents of change beneath the seemingly never-changing world that they inhabited. Each day had its own rhythm, as did each month and season, the years made up of interlocking patterns of sowing, growing, threshing and harvesting, patterns that built upon each other, one after the other. Over the months, trucks filled with wheat were replaced with trucks bearing fruit, and then sugarcane, and although the order never changed, the elements of which they were composed always seemed just a little different from the year before. It was always a different truck, a different driver, people she never recognized, in contrast to the people that she knew and loved, who made up the daily mosaic of her life.

'Well, I'm sure you know best,' she said eventually to Mohammad Karim, who had finished his tea by then and was ready to go inside and watch his favourite television programme on the Sindhi channel. This was another novelty in their lives – a channel devoted to Sindhi programmes all day long. They sometimes sat and watched the shows and could not believe what they were seeing – a Sindhi man, a hairdresser, styling the long tresses of a beautiful girl in a modern salon; a young man with a microphone and a box cut out in the shape of a television who would go to all the big cities – Sukkur, Nawabshah, Hyderabad – and persuade people on the street to sing their favourite songs, just like that. These were things that Sebhagi and her husband saw right in front of their eyes but could never fully grasp – people speaking their language but acting in ways that were totally alien to them. It fascinated and horrified them at the same time.

The fact of Sundri's engagement was accepted by all, even lauded. That she was so young made no difference to anyone. It was better for a girl to have her fate decided early, because everyone knew then the sure and certain outcome of events. Besides, it was not unusual in their village for girls to get married as soon as they reached adolescence. They didn't go to school, nor did they receive any training for any job, so there was no point in delaying the inevitable. Sebhagi herself had been married when she was fourteen, and she had given birth to Sundri soon after. The pattern would repeat itself for her daughter, and the women in the village derived some sort of comfort from the fact that this was the way things had always been done.

Sundri showed no reaction when she was told of her engagement. She sucked a strand of hair in her mouth, nodded dumbly at her father when he told her that she had been engaged that day, and then ran off to play with the other children who were romping by the canal. She was still young enough to play with both girls and boys, though in a few years' time she would have to start covering her head with a scarf and stay indoors and help her mother with the chores. But for now, she was still free. It was a freedom that was only temporary, and she was too young to know how precious and fleeting it was, but at least it was not denied to her until the proper time.

Five years later, the day arrived when Sundri was to be wed. Sebhagi recalled all the preparations that had gone into her own marriage, when she had not been much older than her daughter was today. Sundri's wedding dress hung in one corner of the room, blood red and crushed gold, with a matching dupatta that would go over her head, along with fine gold jewellery. The henna had already been painted on Sundri's hands and Sebhagi could see the tracery on her daughter's palms as she lay in her bed, one arm thrown carelessly over her head. It matched the red lines on her feet. A few ubtan massages had been given to the girl in order to make her skin soft and supple for her wedding night. Nothing, though, could take away either the dark sheen on her skin that came from days spent working in the sun, fetching water, feeding the chickens and bringing grass to the goats, or the calluses on her palms that bore testimony to long years of cooking, cleaning, carrying wood and helping with the cotton-picking in the hot summer months.

'Sundri, wake up, wake up,' said Sebhagi, shaking her little daughter awake. 'It's time to get ready.'

Sundri rose from her bed, rubbing her sleep-filled eyes. 'It's so early, Amma. Why do I have to get up so early?'

'You have to take a bath. The water has to be heated. Come on now. Hurry up.'

A few hours later, Sundri was dressed and ready for the wedding. The red and gold outfit was now hanging on her bony frame, which had lost its childhood plumpness and become somewhat angular with the advent of puberty. Garlands of roses around her neck gave the room a sweet fragrance reminiscent of the graves of the Sufi saints that the villagers visited to beg Allah to grant husbands to their daughters.

Still, the girl looked odd, all dressed up in fine clothes and jewellery and new gold shoes. A child in her mother's clothing, or perhaps a doll readied for a tea party by a child who thinks, the more overdone the finery, the more festive the occasion would become. Sundri fidgeted as Sebhagi pinned the dupatta on her head, encouraged by neighbours who had crowded into the little room, laughing, chattering and gossiping.

'It's a fine man she's getting,' said Naseema. This was Sebhagi's sister, whose husband beat her often, but who had still not lost her enthusiasm for the institution of marriage.

'Yes, and I hear he wants to buy a petrol station in two years' time,' added Banoo Mai; Sebhagi did not know much about her, only that she was a widow who had five daughters to raise and seemed put out by the fact that Sundri was being married that day, instead of one of her girls. 'Although I don't think he'll be able to get the money to do it, not with all the debt that his father has incurred in getting him educated.'

'What debt? The school is free,' muttered Sebhagi, pins sticking out of her mouth.

'O, Amma,' cried Sundri as Sebhagi jabbed one of the pins into her head.

'Hush, girl, stop shouting.'

'That's not the only thing that's going to hurt tonight,' screeched Naseema, eliciting a wave of bawdy laughter from some of the women and a mournful tauba, tauba from the others. Sundri looked up at her mother with fearful eyes, and for a moment, Sebhagi allowed herself to feel all the terror and dismay that had been crowding in her heart for months now, ever since the first drop of blood had appeared on Sundri's clothes, signalling the end of girlhood and the beginning of womanhood.

'Allah have mercy, Allah have mercy,' Sebhagi said under her breath. She said nothing to reassure her daughter, but her hands were gentler as she attached the cloth to the girl's hair. 'There – all done now. You look beautiful!'

It was eleven o'clock, and the men were approaching the house now, bringing flowers and sweets for the bride's family. Haji Ghulam and his son, Ghulam Farid, were at the head of the procession, the older man swelling with pride. Ghulam Farid's face was concealed by the flowers that hung from the front of the ceremonial turban, creating a veil to save him from the evil eye. A large necklace made of crisp hundred-rupee notes adorned his chest. The red and white of the notes matched the new white nylon kurta and shalwar he was clad in.

The women inside the house gathered together and began to sing. Some clapped their hands in time to age-old wedding tunes while others shrieked and ululated in the manner of the Arabs who had conquered Sindh six centuries ago. Sebhagi, as the mother of the bride, took her place proudly next to her daughter. Sundri's hands began to tremble but she quickly looked down and kept her eyes downcast. She was sitting on the bed, surrounded by the women, her mother and young girls from the neighbourhood, hands clasped painfully in her lap, her nose still aching from the fresh piercing yesterday. A heavy nose ring was attached by a chain to another trinket in her hair. She had no space to move and could barely breathe in the small, suffocating room. She didn't know what was expected of her, only that all the fuss being made around her seemed to have something to do with her being handed over to another family to live with forever.

The procession of men stopped at the door, where Mohammad Karim was standing to receive them, flanked by his brothers, various cousins, and his eldest son. 'Welcome, welcome to my house,' Mohammad Karim intoned gravely.

'I am honoured to be here,' replied Haji Farid, and they launched into the traditional Sindhi way of greeting, embracing each other, joining their palms together and dipping their heads towards one another. The noise from within the women's quarters mingled with the cheerful din of the arrival of the groom's family in a tumultuous outpouring of joy, because it was surely a joyful day when you welcomed your daughter's in-laws to your house in order to give her to them. This was the reward for the day of mourning that had occurred at her birth. A reward for the days of waiting until a suitable husband was found for her, and the days of fear until the marriage was contracted: the dread that something might go wrong and the promise revoked.

In a daze, Sundri watched as her uncles entered the room where she was sitting with the other women. They asked her three times whether she agreed to the marriage, but of course she was not expected to reply. It was all over in seconds. Once they had finished with the formalities, the women's voices rose in joyful celebration. As the men backed out of the room, Naseema and Banoo Mai, followed by the other women, embraced Sebhagi. Fingers clutched at Sundri's cheeks, bringing her close to countless lips for wet, affectionate kisses. Sundri screamed as they brushed against her newly-pierced nose, which still carried a scab where it had bled slightly after the ring had been forced through it.

'Shush, child,' said Banoo Mai soothingly. 'You will have to bear your pain bravely from now on. This is nothing compared to what having a child will feel like.'

Sundri stared miserably at the faces in front of her. Nobody had bothered to tell her anything about the mysteries of marriage, and she had no idea what lay in store for her, although everyone had hinted at strange occurrences in the night, the agony of childbirth, and various other secrets and rituals which only older married women were permitted to know. Even the advent of her menstrual cycle had terrified her, for her mother had never discussed with her what the bleeding and the pain meant. She had run screaming to her mother. And her mother's forehead had become instantly wrinkled with worry. This had made Sundri think that something terrible was about to happen to her, but her mother had merely shoved some rags into her hands and instructed her to take care of the problem herself. Over the past few months, Sundri had learnt that becoming a woman involved little more than bearing horrors too great to even talk about.

The door opened and Mohammad Karim entered the room, a huge garland of flowers around his neck. 'Mubarak ho, Mubarak ho!' the women sang and chanted as he came in. He accepted the congratulations with a wide smile. Then he glanced towards his daughter, whose face was still downcast.

'Is she ready?' Mohammad Karim asked his wife.

'Yes.' Sebhagi tried not to let the relief show in her eyes, but she could sense that a weight had fallen off her husband's shoulders. He looked as though he had lost ten years in the span of ten minutes. 'Yes. Are they ready to take her?'

'In a few moments. They are still giving out the sweets.'

Sebhagi sat down beside her daughter, who was already no longer hers. She wanted to spend the few minutes remaining between the nikah and the departure, the rukhsati, with the girl she had raised for the past twelve years. She clasped one of Sundri's cold hands in her own and massaged it gently. With her fingers she traced the lines of mehndi that wove pretty pictures of flowers and circles on the small, hardened palm.

'Be good,' said Sebhagi to her daughter, who had already started to cry.

'I will, Amma.'

'Obey your husband. Obey your mother-in-law. Obey your husband's family. Do not bring shame upon our heads. Work hard and have sons.'

'Yes, Amma.'

'He is a good boy. He will look after you.'

At this, Sundri burst into convulsive sobs. 'I don't want to go, Amma, I don't want to go!'

'Silly child! Enough of that! You're a woman now. It's time to go to your husband's family. I don't want to hear any more. Do I have to beat you even on your wedding day?' Sebhagi was mortified. The other women stood around watching the spectacle. Some were crying in sympathy with Sebhagi and Sundri, others were barely able to conceal their amusement. Banoo twisted her lips in a morbid grin, while Naseema dabbed at her wet eyes with the end of her dupatta. Sebhagi took her daughter's chin in her strong fingers and held her face firmly, forcing Sundri to look into her eyes. 'Allah will look after you.'

All too soon, a little group had assembled in front of the house to bid Sundri farewell. Sebhagi stayed with the women, a few steps behind the men, her back straight, her eyes dry. She did not want to show the rest of the village that she was grieving already for the loss of her daughter. Mohammad Karim took Sundri to the front of the procession, a Quran held over her head for protection, and placed her next to her groom, under his protection. The bowed figure of the girl was hidden beneath the chador draped over the wedding finery to camouflage her as she travelled to her new home in the neighbouring village. Suddenly, Sundri looked into his eyes, and for a moment, he felt a pain as sharp as a dagger under his ribs. His breath caught and he couldn't speak for a few moments. Then he braced himself manfully against the ache, and placing a hand on her head, blessed her one final time. Her brother, Abdul Karim, repeated the gesture, and then it was time to go.

The procession made its way to the waiting bus, which had been chartered especially to bring the guests to the wedding. Mohammad Karim watched as his daughter climbed into the bus, helped by Ghulam Farid. Sebhagi had broken away from the wedding guests and stood by his side – something that would raise eyebrows amongst the village women later that day, but for now, he didn't mind. He was filled with sorrow, and it obliterated all normal thoughts from his head. As he watched the bus climb along the artery and make its way to the one-lane highway, he could feel Sebhagi's shoulders trembling next to his. He turned to her and said kindly, 'She will be all right. Don't worry.'

Sebhagi nodded in silent acceptance of her husband's words. In her heart, she knew that her husband didn't know any better than her whether things would be all right for their daughter. But they had to pretend to have blind faith in God, show that their confidence was unshakeable in order to feel that they had a grip on matters that were truly beyond their control. This was the difference between men and women. Women knew from the day they were born how little control they had over anything that went on around them.

They went back to the house, where the celebrations would continue throughout the day. The next day, the men would travel to the neighbouring village for the walima lunch, celebrating the successful consummation of the marriage. The functions were always held during the day because it was dangerous to travel by night; even after the new artery had been built, kidnappings and robberies were still common in that area. The new road just served to bring criminals in from further afield than before.

Sebhagi was looking forward to a day without her husband and son. The women would be gathering at her place for yet another informal celebration. The next occasion would be when Sundri gave birth to a son, and that was at least nine months away, so Sebhagi accepted the work the celebrations entailed for her with silent stoicism and looked forward to the many months of freedom that would follow.

She went and sat with the women. Someone had brought in a drum and was beating out a tattoo to which the women began to dance, raising their arms and parading proudly in time to the beat. Throughout the day, the women of the village would flock to the house, congratulating Sebhagi for having finally achieved the status of the mother of a married daughter. Mohammad Karim and his son sat on the charpai in front of the house, accepting similar congratulations and gifts of money from the men who had not been invited to the wedding. The entire house, small as it was, exuded festivity that, everyone knew, would last late into the evening and spill over to the day afterwards.

Late in the afternoon, when the women were taking a break from the dancing and singing, a sudden scream rang out. It struck Sebhagi's ears like a blow as she stood in the kitchen preparing tea for her guests. The scream came from outside, and she had never heard anything like it before. Her heart began to beat loud enough to be heard in her ears. She stood stock-still in front of the stove while the milk started to hiss and boil. She was paralysed, like an animal caught in the glare of large, cold headlights. When the milk began to boil over, she came to her senses and rushed outside.

Her husband and son were shouting and beating their chests with their own hands. A few men stood curiously around them, watching, while Mohammad Karim's brothers, Sundri's uncles, moaned in unison.

Five strangers stood before the men of her family. Sebhagi recognized them as part of the wedding party that had left barely a few hours ago. Fear shot through her entrails and cut through her heart at the very sight of them.

'What is it? What has happened?' Sebhagi's eyes were wild, seeking answers from her husband. But he was unable to speak. Abdul stopped his self-flagellation and stared at her, his mouth working, but words failed to emerge. By this time, the women inside the house had spilled out into the sunlight, pulling dupattas over their heads and in front of their mouths.

Finally, Abdul spoke. 'It's Sundri… Sundri…'

'What's happened to Sundri?'

'She is dead…'

The words tore through Sebhagi's head and a low moan escaped her lips. The women gasped as one. Some began to keen, while others simply stood there and stared dumbstruck.

'How? How did she die? Was it an accident?' Sebhagi forced herself to ask, through a daze of shock and disbelief.

'No,' said one of the men from Ghulam Farid's village. He was a young man of about the same age as the groom, and the family resemblance indicated that he was a close cousin. The other men stood, arms folded across their chests, their faces grim with the news they had been sent to deliver to the unlucky man and his wife.

'Then what is it? What happened?' Sebhagi shook her husband's arm desperately. This seemed to bring him out of his trance and he looked at her with pure agony written in every wrinkle of his face.

'My daughter... she...' began Mohammad Karim. He sank to his knees and held his head in his hands.

'Tell me!' Sebhagi shrieked.

'She... she was killed. She was declared a kari. They killed her!'

The wind began to rush in Sebhagi's ears, and she almost fell. Naseema reached her just in time and held her tight. Sebhagi willed herself to remain conscious and leaned back against her sister, although every cell in her body cried out for annihilation. 'It can't be true! It can't be. She just got married today. How can this be?'

The young man from the next village stepped forward. The look on his face was one of genuine sadness, but his voice was like steel as he spoke. 'We were told, as we left here, that the girl used to play with the boys in the village before she was married.'

'Who has told you this? They are lying!' said Sebhagi, the tears now running down her face unchecked. She couldn't believe that Sundri, the sullen little girl with the apple-dark cheeks and laughter like the rush of water in a mountain stream, had besmirched anyone's honour, much less that the girl was now dead. To bring dishonour after all, was a sin of the worst kind in the place where they lived, a sin that merited death and only death.

'It was one of the women in your village. She was here for the wedding. She spoke to my uncle. She said that the girl used to play with the boys in the village. The girl was shameless, the woman said. She would laugh in front of them and walk in front of them and make them go mad with lust for her. This was too great an insult for my uncle's family to bear. They called a meeting of the elders and decided that she had to be killed as kari. It was done before the asr prayers.'

Sebhagi stared, uncomprehending, at the man's face. His lips were moving, he was speaking normally, but suddenly she could not hear anything he was saying, as an ocean of grief swelled and broke over her head, submerging her in its depths. She too fell to her knees and began to scream, tearing her dupatta in half. Mohammad Karim resumed beating himself with his fists, and Abdul Karim stumbled away, half blinded, towards the canal, with thoughts of throwing himself into it in order to escape the shame that had descended upon them like a storm cloud of death.

'I believe the woman who accused your daughter has five daughters of her own. She offered one of her daughters to Haji Farid as compensation for this crime, in order that the entire village does not suffer the consequences. My uncle agreed and the marriage is to be contracted in two weeks' time.'

The man from the neighbouring village drew his companions close to him and they began to walk away, towards the bus which only hours ago had brought them for the wedding, and was now taking them home. But not to a funeral. There would be no funeral for Sundri. Dishonoured women like her were left to lie in the streets for hours. They were buried not in consecrated grounds, but in fields far away from any graveyard, without even a tombstone to mark the fact that anyone had been laid to rest there. In this land, not even the bones of the dishonoured were worthy of remembrance.

The Goonga

Qaisra Shahraz

'The goonga is here! The goonga is here!' the village children shouted one Friday afternoon. The mosque in the centre of the village was echoing with the muezzin's call to prayer. Only the women and children were at home. The men – all devout believers – had taken their Friday bath and gone to the mosque to listen to the maulvi's sermon, and to offer the special Friday prayers.

Over the low walls of their courtyards, some women peered out expectantly.

The goonga, their dumb village simpleton, was back in the village. They hadn't seen him for over five years.

The crowd of children swelled as they followed the goonga, a forty-year-old dishevelled looking man with an unkempt beard, carrying a bundle of clothes in the crook of one arm. Mamun smiled indulgently, an idiotic grin coupled with a nervous tic that contorted one side of his face. Two of the older children still remembered him. It was they who had begun calling out 'goonga, goonga', thinking they had the license to address him thus because he looked like a fool, an idiot.

Mamun, still smiling, stood still for a moment in their midst, in the village lane. He peered eagerly at the children's faces – perhaps he was among them!

By the time Mamun reached Nimat Ali's house, word had gone round the village that Goonga was back. Nimat Ali's wife, Amina, had just finished making chapattis in the clay oven when she heard his name. Her heart started to beat rapidly.

By the time the door of the courtyard opened and Mamun entered, Amina was in control of herself.

She smiled and stood up with the words 'Welcome, welcome' on her lips. She used sign language to ask how he was, and then pulled up a chair for him.

The entourage of children, including Amina's, watched in wonder and amusement as the two held a silent dialogue using gestures. They had never come across a person who couldn't speak – it was a novel experience for them.

The goonga was pointing to his chest and making a sign with his hands to Amina.

She understood. Nodding in understanding, and smiling, she pointed to Siddique.

Mamun quickly swivelled his gaze to look at one of the two boys in the courtyard, standing near the concrete pillar holding the veranda in place. Six-year-old Siddique looked back at him.

Of their own accord and much to his embarrassment, tears crept into Mamun's eyes. His heart swelled with pride and love. His Siddique was a beautiful boy now. Without thinking, he got up from the chair and reached towards the boy, wanting desperately to touch him and to embrace him.

Siddique looked up terrified. Before Goonga's arms could touch him, he ducked away in disgust and horror, and ran to hide behind his mother.

The goonga stood near the pillar, his hand on its cold surface, mortified. The rejection by his own son had done what hundreds of other people had failed to do over the past thirty years of his life.

He wanted to get away from the jeering children and hide in some dark corner and bury his sorrow. He felt too bitter and hurt to exchange niceties with Amina and the other village women and the elders, who had once been his dear friends.

Deliberately averting his gaze from Siddique, he left Amina's courtyard, paying no heed to her when she called out to him to stay and have something to eat and meet her husband Nimat Ali. Waving a hand in dismissal over his shoulder, he made his way to his own house.

He ignored the people he met. The sight of Siddique cowering behind Amina was etched on his retina, cutting him to his very soul. The child had turned away from him in fear and loathing. Would he ever acknowledge him as his father?

Amina sat down on the chair with a leaden heart, thoroughly shaken by Siddique's reaction to his father. Her heart went out to Mamun, imagining how he must feel – but what did one expect from a child, she asked herself.

As far as Siddique was concerned, he had no other parents, only Amina and Nimat Ali. He was a member of their family and had been raised by them as their own child, almost like a twin to her own son Rafique. How could Siddique, therefore, be expected to embrace a complete stranger – a dumb man at that?

An hour later, Nimat Ali returned from the mosque.

'Well, well, Amina Bibi, have you heard that our goonga has returned? Has he been in?' he asked his wife. It had never occurred to him to call Mamun by any other name. 'Yes,' replied Amina in a subdued tone. She signalled to him with her eyes not to say any more. She lifted an eyebrow towards Siddique, who sat eating his dinner on the veranda, under the ceiling fan.

Nimat Ali lowered his voice.

'Did he see Siddique?'

'Ssh! Yes, the boy was quite upset!'

'Why?'

'Mamun came in and tried to embrace him. Siddique was afraid of him and took flight. Mamun was very hurt by the boy's reaction and left immediately, without even a goodbye.'

'Poor man! God! How he must be feeling! He has probably been looking forward to seeing Siddique, his precious son, his only living relative and possession.'

'I feel terrible, Nimat Ali. I don't know why. It's almost as if we have done him a great wrong.'

'Oh, come on, Amina Bibi. Don't talk rubbish! If it wasn't for you, the baby wouldn't have survived without its mother.'

'That may be so. But Mamun has been separated from Siddique for so many years, and when he returns, the child rejects him. It's almost as if it is our fault, as if we have usurped his rights as the father.'

'I don't know how your woman's mind works, but you know that we have provided for Siddique and treated him as a son. And you have been the best mother that he could possibly have.'

'Ssh, he is coming.' They stopped talking as Siddique passed them to go out to play in the fields with his school friends.

Mamun sat in the darkness of his little room, in the ruined remains of his humble home. Outside, it had grown dark. The darkness provided the shelter that his heart craved.

He wept for his 'lost' son, his dead wife, and his own speechless existence.

The whitewashed plaster had peeled off the mud-baked walls. His wife's few pots, stacked in one corner, were dusty and strewn with cobwebs. Most of the furniture had disappeared. Not that they had ever had much. There was only a rickety old chair, a canvas backed charpoy, and a footstool in the main room.

Mamun's grey eyes skirted the room in the darkness, as he recalled those days when he had lived here with his wife, Goongi, who was also dumb.

He was lucky to have a wife, he was always told. She happened to be dumb too. For who would give their daughter to a goonga, whose status was the lowest of the low and whose disability was a major stumbling block? In the minds of the villagers, his disability was somehow synonymous with his intelligence, or the lack of it. It was made worse by the nervous tic that marred his face every time he made an effort to mouth words or when he became excited or emotional.

The villagers always found it interesting and amusing to watch Goonga and Goongi communicate with each other in gestures. How did they do it? How did they explain complicated concepts to each other and express their feelings?

The villagers teased them and made the poor unfortunate couple the butt of many jokes. Mamun and his wife Naima tolerated their teasing goodnaturedly, although they chafed within at the overt cruelty. They wore a perpetual mask, a grin for the outside world; without it they were bereft. People assumed somehow that since they couldn't talk, they couldn't feel anything either. It was only the most considerate and perceptive who refrained from patronizing them, or told the children off when they openly made fun of Mamun as he walked down the street, calling him 'goonga, goonga'.

How many times he had whispered silent prayers of anguish to Allah, at the injustice of it all, at being deprived of speech. Without his voice, he was rendered almost half a man.

He still recalled bitterly how women had cast sly glances in his direction when his wife had become pregnant. Somehow, the fact that they were ready to become parents didn't quite tally with the popular image of Goonga. If the women were sly in their teasing, the men were openly cruel. Mamun often wondered how other men would feel if someone talked about their wife's pregnancy in the same vein.

When, at last, his wife bore him a son, the village was agog with delight and surprise. By God, Goonga had a son and not a daughter. Somehow that made him as normal as the next man.

The words 'The goonga has had a son!' resounded through the village like jungle drums. Most of the villagers joined him wholeheartedly in his feverish delight, including Nimat Ali and his wife Amina. Naima worked as a helper in Amina's home. Sweetmeats were distributed in the village. The khusrahs, transvestite dancers, came to dance and celebrate the birth of his son.

Mamun's cheekbones ached from the grin stretching from one ear to the other. He was in and out of his home all day long, and would not leave his wife and son's bedside. Naima too was delighted, though still very weak from the delivery. They were a complete family. They had a beautiful son who cried naturally. The noise delighted the parents. All through the pregnancy, both of them had been sick with worry about the baby inheriting their disability.

Mamun's joy was shortlived. It was almost as if he was fated to suffer a loss. Three days later, his wife died of a uterine haemorrhage and Mamun was stupefied. He wailed. A harsh, ugly ragged noise, it disconcerted the villagers. They wept with him. At times, he went wild. He banged his head against the walls. They tried to restrain him, but to no avail. The sight terrified some of the villagers crowded into his tiny courtyard.

It was the sound of his son's cries that brought Mamun to his senses. Gently picking him up from the bed, he cradled him to his chest until the mite stopped crying. The realization dawned on him that he had a son to see to. The baby kept crying. He rocked it to and fro.

One of the women in the courtyard took the child from him, wondering how to feed it. The goongi had breastfed it for the past two days. They wondered what Mamun was going to do. He had no family. He was an orphan from the next village, abandoned by his relatives. The baby needed a woman's care. How could he, a man, take care of a baby and feed it?

Amina, with a four-month-old son, was amongst the crowd of women in Goonga's home. Her generous heart swelled with pity for Mamun's predicament. Going to the woman who was holding the baby, she took it and moving to one corner of the room, began to breastfeed him, covering herself discreetly with her chador. The baby quietened almost immediately, and a hushed silence fell in the room. They all stared at the woman, with her head bowed over the baby.

Mamun gestured his thanks to Amina. She accepted it and continued feeding the baby. A few minutes later, she returned the child to him. Mamun cradled the baby's face against his own and began to walk back and forth as though in a trance. The village women stepped out of his way, watching with tears in their eyes.

For the first time in their lives, they identified and empathized with their goonga. He was a young man of thirty-three years and his whole world had collapsed around him.

The next few days passed in a daze for Mamun. At the time of the funeral, there was a constant stream of people coming and going. As was the custom, women gathered together to read passages from the Quran. Amina came regularly to feed the baby and change him. Mamun was very grateful to her and he tried to express his gratitude as well as he could, but he also felt bitter. He had always wanted to see his wife breastfeeding their son. It galled him to see his child nestling against Amina's body.

After a few days, Mamun realized that the child should be near Amina, particularly at night when it cried. Also, it would save Amina the trips she made to his home. Mamun did not want to bottle-feed his son, in case he did not take to it and fell ill. Therefore, after two weeks, he took the baby to Amina and beseeched her to keep him in her home; he would visit him there. She promised to look after him as best as she could. She told him he could come anytime during the day to see his son.

After leaving his son with Amina, Mamun stood outside Nimat Ali's house and wept. It was almost as if he had given his son away.

In the following days and weeks, he visited his son regularly, but his visits became fewer and shorter each time. As time went by, he began to feel awkward and uncomfortable when he held his son or stayed with him. It was as if he was the intruder.

Amina noticed his unease and was obliging in every way, whenever he came. She handed him the child who had been named Siddique by her and Nimat Ali. Then she busied herself with her household chores. He noticed, with delight, that the baby was always clean and well dressed, and in clothes that he could never afford.

But the ache in his heart for his wife and the family that he had always dreamt of would not go away. Finally, when he couldn't bear it any longer, he decided to break away from his life in the village and go live in the city. He was slowly being choked to death by his anguish.

One morning, with a leaden heart, Mamun went to see Nimat Ali and Amina. They were very surprised to see him so smartly dressed and with all his worldly belongings in tow.

After eating the breakfast that they offered, Mamun gestured to Amina that he wanted to see his son. She took him inside the bedroom where the baby was sleeping soundly. Mamun stood over the cot for a long time, wanting to pick his son up, but afraid of disturbing him. At last, when he could bear it no more, he broke down and wept.

Seeing him cry, Amina quickly picked up the baby, mindless of his crying at being rudely awakened, and handed him to Mamun.

She gestured to Mamun to sit on her bed with the baby, and then left, closing the door behind her. Mamun kissed his son's face over and over again and held him tightly against his chest. If the child was older, he could perhaps have looked after him, but there was no way he could cope with a four-month-old breastfed baby.

Mamun stayed with his son for over an hour, and with a tear-stained face, indicated that the child was Amina's now. Then he left, signalling his farewell.

Soon after, Amina went to pick Siddique up and gave him a loving hug. Allah was her witness, she would look after this baby better than her own. She found three hundred-rupee notes beside the baby; Mamun had left them behind. It was his way of thanking Amina and Nimat Ali.

That was the last they saw of Mamun, until he turned up again. Apparently, he had worked in different places and had done menial jobs in some large villas in Lahore.

When Amina went to visit Mamun later in the evening to give him some food, she found him huddled on the floor in one corner of his small courtyard, staring into space. She mustered up a cheerful tone.

'Come on, Mamun! What are you doing, sitting in the dark by yourself? Turn the lights on! I expected that you would come and eat! Oye! Mamun!'

Mamun raised anguished eyes to Amina. In the darkness, neither of them noticed a small head peeping into the courtyard behind the door. Siddique had followed his mother, surprised and intrigued that she was visiting the strange dumb man. He stood listening outside, still afraid of the man.

Amina sat on the old footstool, while Mamun continued to stare into space, almost oblivious of her presence. He wanted to tell her to go away, to leave him alone, so that he could bury himself in the past. He was too tired, however, to attempt miming with his hands.

'Mamun, please, don't take it to heart. Siddique is only a small child. He doesn't know anything. He has never seen a dumb person before.'

She had Mamun's attention now. He looked at her. His grey eyes pierced hers. They spoke volumes. Again she found herself wanting to take away some of his pain. She desperately wanted him to excuse Siddique's behaviour.

'Mamun, your son doesn't know that you are his father, otherwise I am sure he would have come to you.'

She was cut short by the sound of running feet. She looked up and then continued. She had no way of knowing that Siddique had just fled from his position of innocent eavesdropping.

When she returned home, she didn't notice anything unusual or miss Siddique at first. It was only later that they began to be concerned. They asked the neighbours whether they had seen the boy. Nimat Ali was on the point of sending out a search party when Siddique sauntered in with a sullen expression on his face. He paid no attention to their expressions of surprise and indignation. When they asked where he had been all this time, he replied that he had been playing. In reality, he had sat behind an old well, out in the fields, his young mind trying to make sense of what he had heard.

He didn't eat anything. He went to bed early, but lay awake until the early hours of the morning. His eyes stared into the darkness. That beggar, that goonga, was his father. It just couldn't be! First, he felt nauseous; then a sense of betrayal welled up inside him. Pride prevented him from confronting his mother about what he had heard. The knowledge alone shamed him. It was better that no one else knew how he felt.

The next morning, Mamun was sitting on a tree stump near the old well, under the shade of a large tree. Children began to gather around him, to stare and make fun of him, gesticulating with their hands in an effort to mimic his actions.

Mamun watched and stared philosophically. They were children. Then he recognised one face in that crowd of children. His body stiffened as if an electric current had passed through him.

The child watched him, his eyes full of hatred. Goonga dropped his gaze. His body began to tremble, the nervous tic in his cheek worked in full force. This was his son. He hated him. And yet the child did not know, could not know, who he was.

Siddique's jeering words, 'goonga, goonga', were full of a venom unusual for a six-year-old. They stripped Mamun of any semblance of human pride or dignity.

He got up from the tree stump and backed away from Siddique and the other children, almost tripping over a large stone. The group, minus Siddique, followed him, still shouting and laughing.

Siddique watched Goonga and the children go. He picked up two pebbles from the ground and threw them into the well. Strangely, he felt better than he had the previous evening.

As he walked home, the look on Goonga's face as he stumbled on the stone flashed before his eyes. It would not go away. He returned home and sat and tried to read some books. Some time later, he heard Nimat Ali tell Amina in a concerned voice that Mamun had left the village again, this time without saying goodbye.

Siddique listened to their conversation intently. When Amina caught his gaze, he quickly averted his eyes and for no reason at all felt guilty, as if he had done something terribly wrong.

After that evening, nobody talked about Goonga, and he never returned.

Years passed and Siddique grew older, but the vision of that man still haunted him – as did the knowledge that he had driven him out of the village. He still harboured the secret of knowing that he was adopted, and he never told his adopted parents that he knew that he wasn't their son. He wanted to know about his own parents, but didn't dare ask. He found out about his mother, the goongi from Amina. Amina described her in such loving, glowing terms that he almost wanted to cry. She even showed him a photo. Often, he would sneak it out of the dresser drawer to look at it. Since then, he had found out where her grave was, and had once or twice visited it on Fridays.

It was an ordinary day like any other when the peace of the village was shattered by the arrival of a truck from town, accompanied by one of the villagers. In the village, the arrival of a truck normally meant either of two things: buffaloes were being transported out, or a corpse was being brought back to the village. It turned out to be the latter this time. The dead man was Goonga.

Within seconds, word spread throughout the village, and men and women came running from their houses.

Amina and Nimat Ali went ahead of everyone else to the truck. Amina was in a terrible state. Her three sons, including Siddique, trailed behind her. The cot on which Goonga lay was ceremonially lifted out by four men, and carried through the narrow village lanes and alleys to Nimat Ali's home. The link between Goonga and Nimat Ali had been established a long time ago.

The cot was placed in the middle of the courtyard and everybody tried to get a closer look at their goonga. They were eager to know what had happened to him. How had he died? He looked so emaciated. Poor man!

Soon they learned that he had led a rough life in the city, moving from place to place. He had fallen sick then. Fortunately, the man who found him in this pitiable condition was a local chap who had taken him to the hospital where Gunga had died of pneumonia.

In the village mosque, the priest made preparations for the funeral to take place the following morning. During the night, a small group of men and women kept phoory, a vigil over the body. They talked, read from the

Quran, and ate. They discussed the poor goonga and his goongi. Although they had teased him in his lifetime, they had nevertheless loved him, and would dearly miss him.

The next day, early in the morning, Mamun's body was carried to the mosque, where it was given the ceremonial funeral bath. His funeral was held in the mosque, led by the priest and attended by a group of men. Mamun's dead body, carried by four men and led by two priests and two village elders, made its way to the graveyard on the outskirts of the village. The procession of women, children and younger men followed.

The women's group was headed by Amina and the men's by Nimat Ali, as was befitting. Soon the group reached the graveyard. The maulvi began to read verses from the Holy Quran.

The burial over, the men turned away from the grave to head back to the village when something very strange happened.

Siddique, to everyone's amazement, ran towards the grave, fell on his knees and began to wail at the top of his voice. His cries shattered the sombre atmosphere, shocking and disconcerting everyone around him. Did this mean that Siddique knew that Goonga was his father?

Nimat Ali and Amina were heartbroken. They realized that Siddique must have known that they were not his parents. Their heart leapt to their son's anguish as he bent low over the grave.

Amina gathered him in her arms and hugged him. Siddique moved out of her arms, clawing her fingers away.

'Leave me alone.' He looked up and saw people staring at him as he bent over the grave.

'Stare away, everybody! That's what you always did to him, didn't you? Your dear Goonga whom you so loved to tease and make fun of! Well, I am your Goonga now. I am his son!'

His gaze skittered over the faces of the villagers. He spat out the next bitter words that spilt from deep inside him – he didn't know from where.

'Yes, I am his son. Like the other children, I too called him names and jeered at him. It was I, his son, who drove him away from the village.' His words stumbled over the lump in his throat, almost choking him. 'I'll never forget the look on his face when I called him names. He was my father!'

He turned to glare at the astonished group facing him and waved his arms towards the grave.

'Here, everybody, look, this is my father. I, today, am his mouth, his voice, his son. A son he had to give away and later disown entirely because his son discovered him instead. I will not let anyone say anything against my father. Do you hear that, all of you?' He stopped short, his body racked with sobs. Some villagers cried with him.

After the funeral was over, he returned home with his mother. Later, wordlessly, he left home and went to his father's home, and there he lay on the charpoy, the bed on which his mother had given birth to him. Amina and Nimat Ali knew where he was, but they did nothing to bring him back. It was as though they lost not only their Goonga but also their son on the very same day.

That Heathen Air

Muneeza Shamsie

'I wish I had died rather than see this day,' said Princess Gohar Taj. Wrapped in a light shawl, worn over a long shirt and clinging churidar pyjamas, she paced up and down her bedroom. For the first time, God had failed her. Her prayers had brought neither peace nor comfort. Her small bejewelled fingers touched the heavy drapes over the French windows. She fidgeted with the latch.

'Open this,' she commanded her maid.

Her diaphanous dupatta slipped off her head as she stepped out into the airy veranda of her modern, westernized home.

Princess Sultan Jehan followed her out. She was Gohar Taj's youngest sister, and had come to Delhi to give moral support. She leaned her head against Gohar's, her long dark plait falling at an angle to her sister's.

'I marvel at your courage,' she said.

'Courage?' Gohar's voice echoed. 'I don't have courage. All I have is a broken heart.'

In the garden, a huge tamarind tree spread its branches across the pale sky of Delhi. The British, having won their war against the Germans and vanquished the Kaiser, were now building their new imperial capital, New Delhi. The air was filled with the wild clamour of birds, and the scent of overblown roses.

'Of course, I knew that I would have to face this,' Princess Gohar Taj said. 'He told me so, many years ago. That is why he hired an English governess for the children.'

Princess Gohar Taj, being a woman of the royalty, never referred to her husband, Justice Sir Akbar Ali Khan, by name. He in turn called her Begum, which meant Lady.

'People say that the English have become masters of India because they are brought up in a cold invigorating climate,' said Princess Sultan Jehan. 'The water they drink there is very beneficial apparently, so is the food. We Indians have been debilitated by all the spices and chillies we eat, and the hot climate.'

Sultan Jehan was fifteen and had been married for three months. She was quoting her handsome, aristocratic husband, Sahibzada Mahboob Ali Mirza, who had travelled the world over, accompanied by his Persian, English and Indian tutors. He had often spoken to her of Europe, its spirit of inquiry, its spotless, lamp-lit cities, its great factories spewing out wonders: it was another century, another time. But he had expressed his abhorrence for a strange band of abnormal women there who demanded equality with men.

'The English are inhuman monsters,' Gohar Taj burst out. 'No normal being can equal their intrigue, cunning or cruelty. That is why they rule India. And for no other reason.'

For a moment, she forgot that in the social circles of imperial India, she was the gracious Lady Akbar Ali Khan, one of the first Muslim women to discard the veil, learn English and entertain the Viceroy and Vicereine, governors and princes. She was conscious only of the fact that she was a descendent of Bahadur Shah Zafar, the last Mughal Emperor of India.

Princess Gohar Taj had grown up on tales of British atrocities during the Ghadar of 1857. She knew exactly how the British had hunted down and murdered the men of her family – the imperial princes – and displayed their dead bodies naked by the Khooni Darwaza, the Bloody Gate. They had raped the women too, or given them to their Indian allies as slaves or booty. Her grandmother was fortunate to have escaped, but she had never forgotten the red-haired, red-faced Englishman who had ripped her ruby and pearl earrings off her earlobes.

In 1858, the British convicted the Emperor for treason. They exiled him with a small retinue to Rangoon. But Princess Gohar Taj's grandfather had been luckier than most because, influenced by his father, the poet-Emperor, he had taken up calligraphy as a hobby. This enabled him to eke out a living by producing beautiful hand-written copies of the Holy Quran, and to rent a tiny room in Delhi, the erstwhile Mughal capital. There, he and his family continued to be addressed by their imperial titles. For years, no one thought it necessary to tell Princess Gohar Taj that after her grandfather's death, her father, having little income, had accepted a lucrative offer to teach Persian, Urdu and Arabic to scholarly Englishmen.

One day, she discovered that her brother was going to join the Anglicized Muslim University of Aligarh. Her father tried to talk to her about the changing times. He explained that Delhi's old families would only destroy themselves if they refused to learn English. They had to come to terms with the British presence in India. 'Never!' she had cried. Never would she accept the British. Why, if she ever saw an English face, she would spit on it.

A year later, at the age of thirteen, she learnt that her father had given her in marriage to an eminent lawyer. He belonged to 'respectable' stock, which had remained loyal to the British during the Ghadar, but his parents held Gohar Taj's Mughal lineage in high regard. They wanted neither wealth nor riches. They were content with the great honour of being linked to her family name. The bridegroom, Akbar, was clever, important and sober. He enjoyed the confidence of Englishmen and Indians alike. Nothing could stand in the way of his future. Everyone thought she was very lucky to get such a match but Gohar Taj did not think so. Nevertheless, she resigned herself to fate, since she could not express any opinion on her marriage.

Princess Gohar Taj learnt English. She learnt to mix with Englishmen and Englishwomen with a smile. She learnt to tolerate English governesses and her husband's English ways.

'Today, he will be taking Jafar away from me,' she said. 'He is sending my eldest son, my little, ten-year-old boy to school in England. After a few years, he will send Javaid, the younger one, too. To imbibe that heathen air, and that water which has made them masters of India, and which will alienate my sons from me forever. They will probably become Christians and marry English women, for all I know!'

She hated her husband for it.

She saw herself burying him in the sea that was to separate her from her son.

She wished him dead.

She could only be grateful that in this westernized home of theirs, her husband did not find it necessary to retreat to the women's apartments, since there weren't any. He had bought the house from an English merchant. He had renovated an entire suite for himself, based on some grand house he had seen in England. He only came to her when the mood so took him, which was rare. He was usually too exhausted after his day in court.

Princess Gohar Taj prayed that Allah would not give her any more sons.

'I wonder if Englishwomen cry for their children as we do?' said Princess Sultan Jehan. She led a virtually segregated life still, and lived with her in-laws in a princely state. She had little contact with the English.

'Why should they?' retorted Gohar Taj. 'Do you think they're human? Do you think it matters to them that their little ones are sent away at the age of six, or seven or eight? They call that ungodly country "home". They extol its virtues and disparage India all the time. I have to pretend to be too stupid to notice.'

She was glad that at least she had one daughter, Roshan Ara. She would remain in India, but Roshan Ara was now eleven and betrothed. It was only a matter of time before she reached puberty and was taken away from her mother, to her new home.

'He is so small, my little Jafar,' she wept. 'He's only ten. How will he manage in England, all by himself? Among all those strangers? Oh, why does his father want to send him now? Why can't he wait, like everyone else? And send him later? When he finishes school?'

'He wants Jafar to be equal to any Englishman,' said Sultan Jehan. She was filled with sudden panic. What if the Judge Sahib persuaded her husband to send her little sons away to England too? She added, 'I suppose men think that sort of thing is more important in this day and age than a mother's love.'

'No one will ever convince me of that,' Gohar Taj answered.

She stepped inside and glanced at the clock of gilt and lapis lazuli on the carved mantelpiece. It was almost time to go and meet the children. She resisted the temptation to run into the nursery and hug her son. She knew Miss McBride, the governess, would not approve of the breach in routine. She could only meet her children for an hour after breakfast and two hours at tea-time. There was no question of the children leaping onto her bed, or snuggling into her bedclothes, as in any normal home.

'It's time for your bath,' Sultan Jehan reminded her.

'Yes,' said Gohar. She summoned her maid with a silent gesture. 'Yes. I know.'

There would be many visitors to see Jafar off, including some English people. Her husband would expect her to look her best, as always. She curled her hair to fall in waves on either side of her forehead and tied it back into a neat bun. She exchanged her traditional shirt and pyjamas for more "progressive" attire: a high-necked blouse of imported lace, a coordinating imported sari, English stockings and dark high-heeled pumps. With it, she wore the modern jewellery her husband had brought from Europe: diamond eardrops, a matching bracelet, a few strings of pearls and an oblong Viennese brooch which affixed her sari to her shoulder.

'How lovely you look!' said Sultan Jehan with rapt admiration. She was a small delicate girl and without vanity. She marvelled as always at her sister's fair, classical features, and the grace with which she wore a sari. Princess Gohar Taj's almond-shaped eyes suddenly filled with tears.

'Sultana.' She seized her sister's hand. 'Sultana, never allow your husband to be influenced by him. Make him promise to you today. Before your children are born. That he will never send your sons away to school in England.'

Sultan Jehan trembled. She worshipped her husband, and was three months pregnant already. 'I dare not offend him by making such a demand,' she said.

The two sisters hugged each other silently.

Princess Gohar Taj covered her head with her sari, as befitted the anglicized Lady Akbar Ali Khan. She made her way down the cool tiled corridors to her son's nursery.

'Good morning, Mother,' her children Roshan Ara and Jafar chorused in English. They bowed then, and said 'Adaab' and performed the traditional salaam. Her eyes swept over them. Her baby boy, Javaid, was curled up in the ayah's lap. Her pretty daughter Roshan Ara had pink ribbons in her short hair, but now that she was older, she had mercifully given up English dresses for decent Indian clothes. Jafar, who was well-built and fair, could well have been an English boy in his Eton collar. His eyes, she noticed, were very large and round. His long, sensitive face was ashen. She was sure he had been crying. Not that she could enquire. The big bustling Miss McBride would not approve.

'Are you packed and ready?' she asked her son softly in Urdu. She always spoke to her children in her mother tongue, although it was forbidden in the nursery. This was her one consistent act of defiance.

'Yes, Mother,' her son answered in English. His voice quivered. He fought back the tears that threatened to shame him.

'Oh! My son!' cried Gohar Taj. She was unable to contain herself any longer. She held him tight and wept.

'Begum.' A deep voice resounded from the doorway. 'What's all this?'

A gross malignant shadow fell across the room.

It was he, of course. Her husband. He stood there in his dark English clothes, his feet apart and his hands behind his back. His monocle caught the sunlight and glinted.

'Oh please, don't take him away.' Gohar Taj suddenly broke down. 'Oh huzoor, oh sahib, please don't send him there! Please!' She fell on her knees. She was conscious of the indignity of it. 'Please!'

She had never, ever, debased herself thus.

A shocked Princess Sultan Jehan tried to whisper words of comfort and help her to her feet. Her son and daughter tugged at her clothes. They were confused and frightened.

'Sultana,' rasped Sir Justice Akbar Ali Khan. 'Will you leave Gohar Begum alone?'

Princess Sultan Jehan fumbled, afraid. The Judge regarded his wife and her sister with contempt. They were a pair of stupid silly creatures, he thought. They could learn a lesson or two from the very Englishwomen they criticized. No Englishwoman, he believed, would disgrace herself with such a vulgar display of emotion.

'Oh please...' Princess Gohar Taj held her hands out in supplication.

'Have you taken leave of your senses?' her husband barked. 'Have you any idea what you look like? How you revolt me? And the very child you want to cling to so selfishly – do you think you are a fit mother for any son?'

He seized his son's hand and dragged him away.

Gohar Taj fainted.

She had no idea how long she lay there on the cold floor or who picked her up. When she opened her eyes, she was lying in her bed, surrounded by anxious women.

Her sister wanted to send for a lady doctor, but her husband would not hear of it. He had no intention of pandering to her tantrum, he said. He had already been compelled to compromise his conscience and lie on her behalf, by saying she had a fever. And no, he could not let her enter the drawing room or send Jafar to her to say goodbye. She had done enough damage.

Princess Gohar Taj lay there in a stupor, watching the clock tick by. She heard the carriages drive away. Her husband would never take her to England with him to visit her son, and Jafar could not undertake the long sea voyage to India until he had left school. How would she keep in touch with him? Would he start to think of her as ignorant because she could only write simple English? And would she ever master those tomes by Thomas Hardy, Charles Dickens, Rudyard Kipling and William Shakespeare, which held him in such thrall? Her soul could only respond to the lyrical, mystical poetry of Urdu, which his governess considered a lesser language and which he could hardly read.

Princess Sultan Jehan curled herself around Princess Gohar Taj's back, as she had when she was a child. Her tears soaked into her elder sister's shirt. She remained in the room with her until her husband, Sahibzada Mahboob Ali, returned from dinner with his friends and sent for her.

'Lord,' Princess Sultan Jehan said shyly to her husband, late that night, as she undid her long plait and let her hair fall down to her waist. 'Will you promise me something?'

A heaviness lay on the house. Jafar was half way to Bombay by train, accompanied by his father; Princess Gohar Taj was under sedation.

'Anything,' he said. He was dressed in an embroidered shirt of fine muslin and cotton pyjamas; his shirt was open at the neck to reveal the sparse hair on his chest which he liked her to touch; his elbow rested elegantly against a velvet bolster. A full moon illuminated the garden below, except where the tamarind tree cast uneven shadows.

'Promise me that you'll never send my babies to school in England,' she said.

Her husband paused for a moment. He had soft sensual lips, dark enigmatic eyes, and a cleft which ran across his chin. He gazed at his wife indulgently, threw his head back and laughed. His breath carried a whiff of that English poison, whiskey.

He didn't even think she deserved an answer.

Notes on the contributors

Kiran Bashir Ahmad was born in Karachi, Pakistan. Her articles and poems have been frequently published in Shehri-CBE's newsletter. Her story 'Parched Earth' has been published by the British Council and Oxford University Press as part of the *I Belong* International Story Chain Project. A short film has also been made on the same.

Nikhat Hasan was born in Buland Shehr, U.P. She studied in the Girls' College of Aligarh Muslim University, St. Joseph College, Karachi, and Karachi University. Her literary career began in the 1960s. She lives in Karachi.

Baidar Bakht is an engineer who builds bridges for a living and translates Urdu poetry as a passion. His collaborator, Dr. Kathleen Grant Jaeger (b. 1927), has now retired from teaching and research in English literature at King's College University, Halifax, Canada.

Zahida Hina is a well-known Urdu writer and journalist. Her weekly column in the Urdu daily *Jang* has been running for twelve years. Born on October 5, 1946 in Sasaram, Bihar in India, she migrated with her family and now lives in Karachi. Some of her important works are: *Quaidi Saans Layta Hay*; *Rah Mein Ajal Hay*; *Na Junoon Raha, Na Pari Rahi*; *One Fine Morning in the War* (translation), *Salomi* (translation), *Trenchment Creek* (translation) as well as scripts for numerous plays and serials for television. She has received the Faiz Award as well as the Sagar Siddique Award and the Satoor Award.

Sami Rafiq teaches English at the Aligarh Muslim University and writes poems, stories and features under the pen name Sami un Nisa Asim. She was educated at St. Mary's Convent, Naini Tal, Scindia Kanya Vidyalaya, Gwalior, and Aligarh Muslim University. She has been regularly translating fiction from Urdu into English. Her first novel *The Small Town Woman* can be accessed on BookNetIndia.com

Khaleda Hussain started writing fiction in 1963 under her maiden name. Her stories 'Hazar Paya' (The Millipede) and 'Savari' (The Wagon) stories are charged with a feeling of menace, alienation and loss. She has published three volumes of short stories.

Baran Rehman teaches Critical Theory and Drama in the Department of English at Jamia Millia Islamia, New Delhi. She has an M.A. in English Literature from Allahabad University and a Ph.D from Jamia Millia. Her areas of interest include gender studies, literary theory and translation of fiction from Urdu to English.

Sabyn Javeri-Jillani was born in Pakistan and has lived in England and North America. Her fiction has appeared in various anthologies and literary journals and most recently in *The London Magazine: A Review of Literature and the Arts*. She is currently a Masters student at Oxford University, reading English and Creative Writing.

Soniah Naheed Kamal graduated from St. John's College Maryland, US with a B.A. Honours in 'The Great Books' programme. Her thesis *On Prince Charmings*, *Frogs*, *Love Marriages and Arranged Ones* was awarded the 1996 Susan Irene Roberts prize. Since then her fiction and non-fiction has been published in Pakistan, Canada, India and the US. Her story 'Papa's Girl' is included in the anthology *A Letter from India* (Penguin India) and 'Runaway Truck Ramp' appears in *And the World Changed* (Women Unlimited).

Sorayya Khan is the author of *Noor* (2003) and the forthcoming *Five Queen's Road* (Penguin India, 2008). She has received the Fulbright award and Malahat Review Novella Prize. She lives in Ithaca, New York.

Maniza Naqvi is the author of three novels, *Mass Transit* (OUP, 1998), *On Air* (OUP, 2000) and *Stay with Me* (Sama, 2004). She is working on her fourth novel, *A Matter of Detail*. She was born in Lahore and lives and works in Washington, DC.

Nayyara Rahman is a business student in Karachi. She contributes to *Mag The Weekly*, *Hiba*, and some online forums. Her short story 'Clay Fissures' was one of the five winning entries in a national competition organized by the British Council, Pakistan; the stories were subsequently brought together in an anthology called *I Belong*. Her work was also included in an anthology, *And The World Changed*, published by Women Unlimited India, and edited by Muneeza Shamsie.

Sehba Sarwar's first novel *Black Wings* was published in 2004 (Alhamra Publishing) and her essays, poems and stories have been published in the US, India and Pakistan. She currently lives in Houston (USA) and returns home to Karachi for literary inspiration. (www.sehbasarwar.net)

Bina Shah is the author of *Animal Medicine* (OUP 1999), a collection of short stories for children, and two novels: *Where They Dream in Blue* (Alhamra 2001) and *The 786 Cybercafe* (Alhamra 2004). Educated at Wellesley College and the Harvard Graduate School of Education, she is based in Karachi where she freelances for newspapers and web sites. This short story is taken from her new collection, *Blessings* (forthcoming).

Qaisra Shahraz is a prize-winning novelist, playwright and Fellow of the Royal Society of Arts. Born in Pakistan, she lives in Manchester (UK). Her novels *The Holy Woman* (winner of the Golden Jubilee Award and Best Book of the Month) and *Typhoon* have been translated and published in various countries including Holland, Turkey, Pakistan and Indonesia. Her drama serial *The Heart is It* won two TV Awards. Her award-winning short stories are studied in schools: 'A Pair of Jeans' has become prescribed reading in Germany. She is also a teacher-trainer and a college inspector for OFSTED and Adult Learning Inspectorate.

Muneeza Shamsie was born in Lahore, educated in England and has lived in Karachi most of her life. She has edited two anthologies of Pakistani English writing, *A Dragonfly In the Sun* (OUP, 1997) and *Leaving Home* (OUP, 2001). She is now writing a book on Pakistani English Literature. She contributes to *Dawn, She, Newsline* and an internet encyclopedia www. litencyc.com. She was a 1999 Fellow of the Cambridge Seminar on *The Contemporary British Writer*.